KV-190-860

WITHDRAWN AND SOLD
BY ORDER OF THE
KIRKLEES COUNCIL

JUDI JAMES

Fashion Features Double Page Spread

DRAGON

KIRKLEES LIBRARIES
MUSEUMS & ARTS

ACC. NO.

CLASS

DEPT.   CHECKED

Dragon
An imprint of the Children's Division
of the Collins Publishing Group
8 Grafton Street, London W1X 3LA

Published by Dragon Books 1987

Copyright © Judi James 1987

British Library Cataloguing in Publication Data
James, Judi
   Double page spread. – (Fashion features; 2)
   I. Title
   823′.914[J]   PZ7

ISBN 0-583-31099-0

Printed and bound in Great Britain by
Collins, Glasgow

Set in Times

All rights reserved. No part of this publication may
be reproduced, stored in a retrieval system, or
transmitted, in any form, or by any means, electronic,
mechanical, photocopying, recording or otherwise,
without the prior permission of the publishers.

This book is sold subject to the condition that it
shall not, by way of trade or otherwise, be lent,
re-sold, hired out or otherwise circulated
without the publisher's prior consent in any
form of binding or cover other than that in
which it is published and without a similar
condition including this condition being imposed
on the subsequent purchaser.

1
Rolling in the Aisles

Carl Curt tapped his right foot impatiently, drumming out a matching tattoo on the crown of the grey top hat he was clutching as he waited for his bride to appear. A small muscle on the side of his cheek started to twitch in time with this miserable little combo as Carl checked his Rolex for the twentieth time that minute.

Only forty-three seconds to go – what did that stupid fat twerp think she was playing at, making him wait around like this? Probably trying to cram all that claustrophobic cellulite around her hips into some snake-sized designer rag, he supposed, tutting as loudly as possible and nearly dislocating his tongue with the effort.

As the first few notes of The Wedding March boomed out of loud speakers concealed high up in the marble pillars that surrounded them, Huw Logg – the hulking six-footer who'd been given the job of Best Man – decided to stir up a little more fun by leaning across and yelling out a countdown.

'Ten! . . .' Carl fingered his too-tight collar then swore loudly when he saw the make-up that had come off on to his powder blue gloves.

'Nine! . . .' The organist thundered on regardless like some hammy extra from a horror movie, totally oblivious to the sound of blood pressures rising above danger level amongst Carl and his cronies.

'Eight! . . .' Carl thought about passing out in a dead swoon.

'Seven! . . .' Carl considered nutting his Best Man instead.

As Huw threw his head back to bawl out the number six, Carl raised his fist menacingly. Huw, however, was a Clint Eastwood groupie. 'Go ahead punk,' he drawled, surveying Carl through eyes that had turned into slits, 'make mah day! . . . Six!'

But suddenly the bride had appeared, looking so young and saucer-eyed and beautiful that, despite the plaster bird's nest on top of her head and the massive bunch of plastic grapes that trailed down her long slim neck and over one shoulder, Carl felt his anger evaporating and he rushed across to aim a kiss at her purple-blushered cheek. 'Ready darling?' he murmured, accidentally nuzzling the stuffed dove that clung to one of her shoulders like Long John Silver's parrot. The bride nodded vigorously, making the plastic grapes jangle wildly.

Taking one of her small hands in his own and chaffing it gently to stop the trembling, Carl inspected his bride's pale face closely. 'This is your first time, isn't it?' he asked, suddenly full of concern.

'Yeah,' the girl replied in a loud wobbly squeak. 'Is it that obvious? I told 'em I'd done it loads of times before. I thought I was doing alright so far.' A small tear of panic appeared in the corner of her right eye.

'Don't worry,' Carl said, smiling, 'the first time is always the worst – soon there'll be no holding you and you'll be able to look back on today and laugh about it. C'mon!'

As Carl tried to lead his still-quivering bride towards the entrance, though, he felt her tug his sleeve urgently. ''Ere, 'ang on a min, Carl,' she shouted, screeching to a halt and fumbling wildly in a small silk

6

bag she was clutching. 'I forgot ter check me batteries in all the rush!' Carl stared in horror as his blushing bride pressed a switch in her hand and the entire enormous bridal bouquet she was carrying suddenly lit up in a twinkling haze of bright green flashing fairy lights. Reassured, she smiled broadly and stuffed the switch back into her bag. "S'okay,' she announced. 'Just checkin'.' She snuggled back into the sleeve of Carl's £3,000 hand-stitched morning suit and at last they seemed ready to roll.

Huw, however, had other ideas. 'I say, mate,' he bawled, throwing himself into their path and grinning smugly into Carl's face, 'd'you know your flies are undone?'

Carl faltered for one milli-second then smiled back confidently. This was an old trick – one of the oldest gags in the book, in fact, and he had no intention of falling for it. 'Good!' he announced, smiling. 'Give the audience something to applaud then, won't it? Now shove off, spamhead!' and he swept past his Best Man feeling extra smug at the expression of shocked surprise that flitted across Huw's smarmy face.

As Carl strode manfully forward, his bride, who hadn't heard the 'your-flies-are-undone' wind-up before, looked down in alarm and found to her horror that, for the first time in his chequered career, Huw Logg had actually been telling the truth. The gap in the front of Carl's trousers was yawning as wide as The Grand Canyon, and was almost as wide as Carl's cheesey smile. The brain that lurked beneath the plaster bird's nest wasn't a particularly bright one, but eight months' work experience at the Co-op in Croydon had taught the girl to think on her feet and, in a moment of divine inspiration and near-blind panic, she

7

took her huge green flashing bouquet and stuffed it, still twinkling, down the front of Carl Curt's charcoal-grey pure wool trousers.

Geraldine Foster-Brown, elegant fashion editor of *Visage*, the high-fashion glossy magazine, sprawled and sank even lower in her front-row seat at the fashion show, paying far more attention to the lumps of soggy, colourless fruit she was carefully fishing out of her free 'press-only' Pimms than she was to the models cavorting on the catwalk in front of her. One chunk of fruit in particular had caught her attention and she held it up to the light for inspection. 'Banana?' she wondered, squinting at it as a £15,000 ranch mink coat flashed past in a hairy blur. 'Nectarine?' Geraldine sniffed the thing cautiously and tried its texture with her teeth. There was no way she was going to swallow it – not until she reached some form of positive identification, anyway.

Sweating it out under the spotlight, the compere of the show watched Geraldine, mesmerised, as she spat something revolting-looking back into her glass and proceeded to prod around with her orange stick like a whaler clutching a harpoon. A sob rose in the back of his throat – if Geraldine Foster-Brown was bored with the show then they were sunk. She'd yawned through the ski-wear, dozed fitfully through the entire ballgown sequence, actually snored during the artistically-cho-reographed sequinned-swimwear routine, and now she seemed to be practising some sort of regurgitation ritual throughout the furs. Boredom was contagious and now the entire press section appeared to be follow-ing suit and either nodding off, or writing shopping lists, or something equally absorbing.

As a quartet of models hit the stage dressed up like blue-rinsed beavers with dead skunks on their heads and proceeded to shuffle about in time to the strains of 'The Harlem Shuffle', Geraldine yawned loudly, stretched like someone waking up out of a coma, and leaned towards the next seat to yell in her daughter's ear. 'I told you Mo Polo was all washed up this season!' she bawled. 'This stuff is all just a heap of pretentious garbage! Worse, in fact – I'd rather sort through Mo's dustbin than look at this lot!'

Seraphina blushed scarlet – her mother's voice had carried well over the loud music blasting from the speakers and people around them were either tutting tetchily or nodding in agreement. Seraphina was also amazed at her mother's gall – up until the show had started she'd been tearing around London telling everyone who would listen that Mo was the sharpest new designer since Jasper Conran.

As the music changed to the '1812 Overture' and models started arriving with sparklers sizzling in their hair, Seraphina squirmed in her hard seat and sighed. She'd come to accept these sudden dramatic changes of taste and fashions since she'd started working for a trial period at *Visage*. She was also uncomfortably aware that the trial period as junior assistant was quickly coming to an end, and if she didn't come up with some interesting work soon the permanent job would go to either Jeremy or Caroline, her two friends and rivals. So far she just seemed to be tagging at her mother's heels like some prize poodle, watching an endless stream of fashion shows, shoots and interviews, while the only really good feature she'd managed to write had been turned down by Dottie, the editor, on the grounds that it offended one of the magazine's

9

biggest advertisers. Seraphina knew that, Geraldine's daughter or not, her head was on the block.

As though reading Seraphina's thoughts, Terence Thomas, the freelance photographer who did most of the work on *Visage*, dug her gently in the ribs and gave her a wink and a grin. Unfortunately Geraldine caught this small sign of affection out of the corner of one heavily-mascara-coated eye and bristled angrily. She couldn't see what her beautiful elegant blonde-haired daughter could possibly see in a male-chauvinist scruff-bag like Terence, but whatever it was, Geraldine certainly didn't approve. 'Terence "Tripod" Thomas may be a bloody good photographer,' she muttered, 'but he is worse than scum when it comes to his behaviour with women.'

Up until the day he clapped eyes on Seraphina, Terence had been a second-generation member of the Warren Beatty/Richard Gere school of manhood, groping and grabbing his way through the never-ending supply of models that blew into his studio, chatting up anything that crossed his path during the day that had no Adam's apple or facial hair, and calling all women 'darlin'' or 'doll', whether they were nineteen or ninety. He still made jokes about girls who lived in Bristol and his idea of culture was to go and see something like 'Porky's Revenge'.

All that had changed however, the day he had spotted Seraphina quietly sipping Perrier in 'The Squinting Pig' wine bar. Terence had fallen hook, line and sinker, and could now be found discussing meditation over a glass of prune juice and a tofu-burger just as happily as he used to compare the assets of various page three girls over a pint of lager and a packet of pork scratchings. Geraldine Foster-Brown, however, knew how to smell a rat when she came across one, and was still determined to drive a wedge between this hairy-chested medallion man and her willowy young daughter before things started to get too serious between them. She leant across to say something to Terence in the vain hope it might stop him drooling over Seraphina, but even Geraldine's voice was drowned as the first blasting notes of 'The Wedding March' rent the air.

The audience groaned in unison – not a bridal finale! How utterly, totally, toe-curlingly passé! Old Mo must've flipped his lid at last! Unable to stand the embarrassment, someone who looked as though they might work for *Vogue* magazine actually stood up to leave, and for a moment it looked as though the rest of the herd might just follow suit. Arms were being shoved down coat sleeves, chairs were being scraped backwards, last dregs of Pimms were being sucked so hard through straws that it looked as though faces might just cave in, and hands were fishing under seats to retrieve carrier bags containing free 'press-only' Mo Polo designer-toilet-roll-holders. Mo himself watched the whole insulting exodus through a gap in the curtains, trying hard to look inscrutable despite a deep-seated, ethnic desire to go off and commit Hari-Kari.

Suddenly the curtains swung back to reveal Carl and his bride – and the audience stopped in their tracks. As 'The Wedding March' thundered on the couple trod sheepishly down the catwalk, stuffed doves bobbing and quivering and bouquet twinkling and gleaming. For a moment there was total silence as even the organist seemed to be taking a dramatic pause, then pandemonium broke out among the press seats. They'd never seen a groom with flashing flies before, and the recently-emptied seats in the front rows were kicked aside in the mad stampede as photographers crushed around the stage, jostling and elbowing one another to get the best shots.

From behind the curtains Mo Polo's heart gave a little lurch of relief – his plaster and grape head-dress must've saved the show after all. Then he noticed that it appeared to be Carl, the male model, who was getting singled out for the photographers' attention, and curiosity drove him out of his little backstage hidey-hole. Carl was only supposed to be an extra – his suit was just rented from a dress hire shop, not a Mo Polo exclusive show-stopper! Then Mo spotted the flashing bouquet that was dangling precariously out of the front of Carl's trousers and his jaw dropped as he realized that his creative genius had been totally and utterly upstaged. Tears sprang to his eyes and he stuffed a length of curtain into his mouth to quickly stifle the scream he could feel building up. Black spots appeared in front of his eyes as he started to hyperventilate, but as the room swam around his head, Geraldine Foster-Brown's voice floated towards him, cutting through all the other noise in the room as clearly as an air-raid siren, dragging him back to consciousness like a nostrilful of smelling salts.

'Wonderful! Terrific!' Geraldine barked. 'So full of humour, so wonderfully witty! Neon nuptials! Mo's flash of brilliance! Are you getting all this down, Seraphina? I knew Mo had it in him – didn't I say he was the best thing since sliced bread? Eh? Eh?'

Seraphina, meanwhile, was furiously trying to write copy as she was tossed about in a sea of writhing, scrabbling bodies. Every time her notebook swung into view she stabbed at it with her felt-tip, but so far she'd only managed to get down a few lines of misspelt gibberish.

Terence, being one of the tallest photographers in the room, had tried his usual trick of keeping to the back of the crowd to avoid the crush, and then lifting his arms and aiming his camera like a gun, shooting above all the heads. It was a trick he'd picked up from his days in Fleet Street, and he'd often got quite good praise for the results. All this cut no ice with Geraldine Foster-Brown, though. Terence managed to ignore her mouthed insults and hand-flapping from across the rows of chairs, although the message she was trying to get across was glaringly obvious. Incensed, she roared over, bowling chairs over in her wake, and started tickling him under the armpits.

'Get to the front!' Geraldine growled, nudging him with her boney knuckles, 'I want close-ups! This is going in a centre-spread, full colour! Focus properly, you berk! Get in there!' Without so much as a backward glance, Terence waded bravely into the seething throng, not so much to get better shots for Geraldine, though, as to rescue Seraphina, whose head he'd just seen going under for the third time. Crunching smaller photographers underfoot and holding his Nikon shoulder high, well out of harm's way, he set off in Seraphina's direction. Twice he found himself packed in so tightly with other bodies that his feet actually dangled off the ground, and each time he was sure he felt someone pinch his bum.

At last he reached the spot where Seraphina had last gone down and, reaching under a pile of abandoned chairs, he grabbed her arm and managed to pull her out, shaken but intact. Seraphina took several grateful lungfuls of air, then flung her arms around Terence's neck and rewarded him with a smacking great kiss on the mouth. Their teeth clunked together painfully as someone in the crowd barged into them, but Terence didn't mind at all – he was floating on air.

In the slight lull that seemed to follow, Seraphina dived for the back of the room, but then suddenly all hell broke loose again. Carl Curt had been basking and sweating in the limelight for long enough as far as his bride was concerned – Mo had told her that *she'd* be the main attraction of the show, and so far all she'd done was to skulk on the sidelines. Even the bouquet-down-the-trousers had been her idea in the first place, but from the way Mo was moving in with a sickly grin on his chops, taking all the applause from the audience and bowing all over the place, it didn't look as though she was going to get much of the credit for that, either! There was only one thing for it. Whipping the bird's nest off her head she tossed it out into the audience like a frisbee and started to strip.

As Carl paused in his posing to gawp in surprise, the bride ripped the grapes out of her hair and started flicking them one at a time at the press photographers. The doves went next, sailing off into the wide blue yonder with a helping kick from the bride's boot, and then she started on the dress itself. It was at that point that the photographers from the newspapers started to smell a good story, and the crush to the front started all over again.

Realizing he had a battle on his hands, Carl decided to compete and the bouquet went sailing off in the same direction as the stuffed doves, and then the stampede around the stage got really serious. Even Geraldine stopped prodding Terence in the ribs and started to cling on to the camera strap around his neck for dear life.

For one moment Terence thought Geraldine was really trying to throttle him for daring to take out her daughter, and for one, eye-bulging second they stood locked in the throes of deadly unarmed combat. The spell was broken suddenly when another photographer trod on the hem of Geraldine's long, flowing skirt, ripping off the entire back panel. Gurgling with anger, Geraldine spun around to sort him out but, to her horror, she watched as he simply picked the strip of fabric up off the floor and proceeded to clean his camera lens with it. 'Thanks luv!' he shouted cheerily, and re-entered the crowd before Geraldine had a chance to shriek out loud.

At the back of the room Seraphine was just emerging on all fours, crawling out from a writhing field of legs, clutching her notebook aloft like the Olympic torch. Terence pulled out of the front line just as Carl had got to the point where only a pair of black nylon socks and a sad-looking sprig from the flashing bouquet stood between him and an arrest for indecent exposure. 'Give me the Falklands any day of the week,' he muttered between clenched teeth as he unloaded his camera and set off to find Seraphina and her old witch of a mother.

'Sometimes – just sometimes,' he thought, 'this job just doesn't seem worth all the effort.' Then Terence caught sight of Seraphina's blonde head bobbing about in reception and he shot off in her direction, grinning like a two-year-old.

2
Egg Foo-Yong

Geraldine Foster-Brown bolted out into the street as though the hounds of hell were yapping at her heels. Clutching her ripped skirt around her bottom with one hand, she looked desperately round for a refuge and ended up diving into the nearest doorway she could find. Exposing herself to all the other fashion journalists would have been bad enough, but Geraldine had other problems in mind, too. She knew that if any of the others caught so much as one tiny glimpse of the knickers she'd hurriedly jumped into before leaving for work that morning, then her entire reputation as a top-notch fashion editor with her finger right on the pulse of all the passing trends would be in tatters. Only last week she'd had an article published claiming that anyone who *was* anyone in the fashion world wouldn't be seen dead wearing anything under their clothes other than a pair of Mexican wild silk hand-embroidered designer boxer-shorts. Here she was then, only a few days later, sporting a pair of greying nylon Marks and Sparks bikini pants for all the world to see.

Peering breathlessly out of her doorway to see if anyone had followed her, Geraldine paused for a bit, fuming silently. She was a woman who was used to getting her own way, but recently things had been taking a nasty turn, and she somehow managed to blame Terence for most of those nasty turns, too. The thought that her only daughter might lose her job at *Visage* made Geraldine shudder visibly – she knew it

16

would make her a laughing stock among her colleagues. Then she realized that if she wasn't careful, not only would Seraphina end up losing her job, she'd probably wind up marrying that worthless hunk of a photographer into the bargain! Geraldine felt sick at the thought of it.

As she muttered to herself angrily, peeping out of her doorway occasionally to see if any cabs happened to be on the horizon, Geraldine suddenly became aware of small, quiet sniggering sounds coming from somewhere behind her. Turning her head slowly she took in her surroundings for the first time since her great escape from the Mo Polo fashion show.

Just behind her stood a small bamboo counter with a large sign hanging over it, informing Geraldine that she had just stumbled into the 'INKING-POO CHINESE TAKEAWAY'. Mr Poo and his family were lined up behind the counter, smiling respectfully at their new customer, despite the fact that they could see her knickers. Mrs Poo was being kept busy clipping ears furiously to keep the snigger level down as they all stared at the funny English lady.

Geraldine took a deep breath and drew herself up to her full height. Nobody spoke and she realized that they were all waiting for her to make the first move. Her eyes darting furiously around for inspiration, Geraldine finally said the first thing that came into her head.

'Ah . . . ah . . . number . . . ah . . . twenty-two . . . to go, please!' she trilled, trying desperately to hide her knickers with her handbag. The Poos stood, rooted to the spot, still smiling but obviously waiting for more. Geraldine snatched a menu off the counter with her spare hand and saw she had just ordered a pot of tea.

'Oh . . .' she said, 'and . . . er . . . number six . . . and . . . er . . . number forty one.' The Poos still waited expectantly. '. . . and . . . a portion of fried rice!' Geraldine finished hysterically, collapsing into a nearby chair.

To her enormous relief Geraldine discovered she had said the right thing at last. The Poos all nodded in unison and the whole place erupted into an orgy of activity. Everyone pottered off to set about their part of her order, and the colour T.V. on the wall was switched on so that she could watch the test card while she waited. Only the littlest Poo stayed behind to watch, thumb in mouth, as the strange lady with her knickers on show pulled a pen and notebook out of her bag and set about plotting her revenge.

Caroline Southgate, one of Seraphina's two rivals for the permanent job at *Visage*, spat on the sleeve of the old woolly she was wearing and wiped a little clear patch in the grimy mirror outside her flat. The face that peered back at her out of the patch was beginning to look familiar again, and Caroline wasn't at all sure that she minded that one little bit.

When she'd started work at *Visage*, Caroline had been a big, awkward-looking, freckly girl with an unruly heap of flaming red hair and a burning crush on Simon, the handsome young journalist in the flat upstairs. Two months later though, Vanessa Gimlette, the new beauty editor at *Visage*, had transformed her for a make-over feature, and the transformation had been so thorough that Caroline had even won a top beauty title.

Slim, tanned, and with her red hair bleached Saman-tha Fox-blonde, Caroline had hoped that Simon would be a push-over, but somehow she was beginning to get the message that he liked her better as she was before. The funny thing was, she had to agree with Simon – she liked herself better as she was before, too! All the strict dieting had made her snappy and miserable, and when the colour was stripped out of her hair and the chubby bits were slimmed out of her face, she looked about as interesting and as full of character as a Barbie doll.

Tilting her head back, Caroline half-closed her eyes and pouted at her reflection. Amused, she stuck one hand behind her head and started wiggling her hips in a mock Marilyn Monroe take-off. Feeling her sense of humour coming back at last, Caroline giggled out loud and then tried out her Madonna routine. Rolling her ancient Fair-Isle jumper up above her waist to show her belly-button, she strutted up and down the landing, arms high up in the air, pretending to chew gum. 'Papa don't preach . . .' she warbled, and then froze as she saw Simon's face, staring in the mirror behind her.

'Simon!' she cried, wheeling round quickly. 'I didn't hear you come up the stairs . . . I was just . . . that is, I . . .'

'Practising for more beauty titles?' Simon asked, smiling coldly. 'Fine . . . Good for you. You should do well.' And he strode off towards the next flight of stairs. 'I'm sorry if I made you jump,' he shouted over his shoulder. 'It must be these new shoes – rubber soles, you know.'

In her desperation to stop him and explain things, Caroline heard herself calling back to him in the sort of high-pitched theatrical voice that women in Noel Coward plays use to penetrate right to the back row of the stalls, or that girls use when they're shy and nervous

19

and embarrassed, as Caroline was at that moment. 'Rubber soles?' she bawled, trying to lean nonchalantly against the banister rail, missing, and tripping up the first step. 'Oh, what a good idea,' she went on lamely, realizing she had no idea how to finish the sentence, and blushing madly as Simon turned to look hard at her.

There was a pause as he watched her curiously. 'Why?' he said, eventually.

'Well . . .' Caroline began, wishing the ground would swallow her up or the ceiling would fall in or something, 'they're very . . . you know, sensible . . . aren't they? You don't . . . you know . . . slip over, or anything . . .' As an electric pink nerve rash broke out all over Caroline's chest and neck, she looked up again and thought she could detect just the trace of a smile around the corners of Simon's lips. Relieved, she smiled back at him and decided to have a go at explaining things at last.

'Look, Simon, I'm not really cut out for those beauty competition things at all, you know,' she babbled. 'In fact, I was only entered for the one I won as a sort of a joke . . . well, not a joke, really, it was more a sort of undercover job for the magazine, just a one-off . . . a bit like . . .' Caroline wracked her brains for inspiration, '. . . a bit like the sort of stuff you do, really!' she finally said, smiling brightly. 'You know, investigative journalism, and all that sort of thing!' The smile froze on Simon's face and Caroline realized she had put her foot in it yet again.

Suddenly she could feel anger welling up inside her. Just who did Simon think he was, anyway, standing there with a face like an acid drop just because she'd happened to win a beauty contest? It wasn't her fault she'd turned from an ugly duckling into a swan overnight, and if he was so fond of ugly girls, then why was he always dating raving blonde beauties? Caroline peered at him more closely. For all she knew his tan might come from a sun bed and those lovely blond streaks in his hair could've come out of a bottle! Who was he to pass judgement on her make-up and new hair colour?

'I'd ask you in for a coffee,' she said with new-found confidence, 'but I'm afraid I seem to have locked myself out of my flat. I came out to get the milk and the door slammed shut behind me. When you crept up on me I was just amusing myself in the mirror to pass the time until my flatmate came back from the launderette – not posing up for the next beauty contest, as you seem to think!' Caroline brandished the carton of milk she was clutching, to prove her case.

Simon was suddenly all charm and politeness again. 'Well, that little problem's easily solved,' he said, running a hand through his hair. 'I've got a large pot of coffee on the go, but I happen to be right out of milk – why don't you come up to my place and wait there for your flatmate?'

Caroline hesitated, suddenly aware of the holey old woolly she was wearing and the pom-pom slippers she had on her feet. Debbie might be gone for hours, though, and she was getting very bored waiting in the hall. 'OK,' she said, beaming gratefully, 'white-two-sugars, please!'

As Caroline stepped inside Simon's flat, though, her heart dropped. He'd just about managed to rip off the note that was sellotaped to his front door in time to stop Caroline reading it, but she saw enough to know that one of his blonde bombshells wanted to meet him

21

that evening, and from the extravagant kisses that were painted all over it, Caroline guessed that it wasn't a meeting to discuss work. There was a large pile of unopened mail behind the door, too, most of it covered in flowery-looking handwriting.

After all this obvious deluge of feminine adoration, Caroline almost expected to find the lounge stewn with discarded bras and G-strings, but in fact the whole place seemed quite tidy and businesslike. Apart from a modern black teak desk in the corner, which held Simon's typewriter and work papers, the whole flat was a happy hotchpotch of style and colour. Framed black and white press photos hung on the walls along-side reproduction Victorian prints, and elaborate, richly-coloured Persian rugs overlapped modern, geo-metric mats on the bare varnished floorboards. An ancient pine washstand was pushed up against one wall and was covered with books and pots containing enormous dried flowers. Simon waved Caroline towards an overstuffed chocolate-coloured settee in the middle of the room, and as she sank happily into it, he shot off into the kitchen to fix coffee.

'Put a tape on if you want,' he yelled above the noise of the grinder.

Caroline scrutinized the cassette rack and realized her choice of tapes could be important. *Love me, love my music*, she thought, noticing the rack contained everything from Bach to the Bronskis. Trying to shake off her new lightweight image, Caroline pulled out the heaviest-looking tape she could find and pushed it into the machine. It turned out to be some sort of new experimental music that sounded like someone falling over drunk in the percussion section of an orchestra. By the time Simon walked in with the tray the air was full of loud disconnected bangings and crashings and Caroline was having a hard time trying not to double up with laughter.

Heaping the sugar into her coffee, Simon pulled a face. 'Unusual choice,' he said, as the drunk seemed to put his foot through the kettle drum and a chorus of banshees started wailing in the background. 'Wouldn't have thought this was your sort of thing at all!'

Caroline stopped smiling and felt the anger welling again. 'And just what would you think was my "sort of thing"?' she asked, stirring her coffee vigorously. 'Donna Summers?'

'No, no,' Simon said quickly. 'I just imagined you liking something a bit more lively, that's all . . . Janet Jackson, or Prince, or something.'

'This is fine,' Caroline said firmly.

There was an uncomfortable pause as she slurped her drink. 'How's the job going?' Simon asked, eventually.

'That's fine, too,' Caroline said, sounding very formal. 'I'm still on a trial period, of course,' she added, warming to the subject, 'but if I can only write something worthwhile that gets accepted for publication, then I might get taken on full-time.'

'What do you mean by worthwhile?' Simon asked, raising one eyebrow.

'Oh, I don't know,' Caroline sighed, leaning back in her seat and looking thoughtful, 'but *Visage* isn't all fashion and beauty, you know – they do have the odd campaigning feature every month. I'd maybe like to do something on how the beauty business affects the Women's Movement, or interview women who've made it in the city . . .'

'And how will all this women's lib stuff tie in with your new status as a beauty queen?' Simon asked, watching her face carefully. 'Surely it's a bit hypocritical to try and combine the two worlds?'

Caroline sat up straight. 'I told you,' she said, frowning, 'that title was a mistake. I'm not a beauty queen and I've got no intention of working in the glamour business. I was working on an exposé when I won that competition – it all turned into some silly mistake!'

'So you've got your heart set on being a fully-fledged ethical newshound like me, have you?' Simon asked, still watching her face closely. 'Perhaps you see yourself as a champion for different causes, eventually? Promoting the woman's role in society, that sort of thing?'

Caroline had an uncomfortable feeling that she was being backed into a trap of some sort, but for the life of her she couldn't see how. 'Perhaps,' she said, cautiously. 'I enjoy doing fashion, but that sort of thing could be more worthwhile . . .'

'More worthwhile than working as a glamour model?' Simon asked, looking angry.

'Well, yes, of course . . .' Caroline began, but Simon cut her short.

'Look,' he said, standing up and glowering down at her, 'this may be none of my business, but when someone I used to admire and trust for their honesty, openness and freshness of character suddenly seems determined to go out of their way to pounce on me from all sides – just to sit in my flat, drink my coffee and tell me a pack of lies, and then start rabbiting on about how they want to be a writer with ethics and integrity just like me, I find it very difficult to control my temper.'

Caroline's jaw dropped in surprise and she tried to get up, but Simon hadn't finished his speech yet, and she found herself being pushed roughly back on to the settee.

'Now I don't care what you want to do with your life,' he went on, his face reddening with anger. 'Maybe I would've cared, once upon a time, but that was when I used to rent a flat in the same block as a stunning, bubbly redhead who seemed to know what she wanted out of life. Now you could pose naked for *Playboy* for all I care – that's entirely up to you. What I do object to are your so-called leanings towards the Women's Movement, etcetera, while you do it!'

Simon paused for breath after this outburst, and Caroline sprang to her feet, quivering with rage. 'I've told you,' she shouted, 'it was a mistake – I turned the title down! I'm not going into glamour work and I'm not a hypocrite. You're the hypocrite, pretending you only liked me when I was a chubby redhead when you go out with a different skinny blonde every night of the week – look!' she added, pointing to the heap of mail behind the front door, 'you even get fan mail from them, or are you going to tell me they're all overdue phone bills?'

For one moment Caroline thought Simon was going to hit her, but instead he just bent down to his coffee table and picked up a handful of newspapers and magazines. 'Yes, I do seem to attract the blonde model type,' he said, thumbing through the first magazine with annoying calmness, 'and some of them, I must admit, do pose for the papers. However,' he went on, finding the page he was looking for at last and handing it to Caroline, 'they don't seem to feel they have to lie about it – *that's* what I object to.'

Caroline looked down in bewilderment at the magazine Simon had passed her. For a moment the page was a blur in front of her eyes, but then the tears of indignation cleared and she saw what he had been talking about. There in front of her was a page of photographs of a model in a miniscule bikini doing some really cheesey-looking poses. It was a few seconds more, though, before Caroline realized that the model in all the photos was her – she was looking at pictures of herself!

Simon threw a newspaper on top of the magazine. It contained one large shot in the same bikini, although the pose was different. 'Curvy Caroline . . . ' the caption ran underneath, '*is displaying all her charms in this summer's hottest bikini. As she tans up for all her latest modelling assignments the bikini may keep Caroline cool, but it'll do a lot to raise other temperatures on the beach this year!*'

Simon tossed another couple of magazines in Caroline's direction as she looked at him in total amazement. 'Hot stuff, eh?' he said with heavy sarcasm.

Caroline stared at the photographs, then she stared back at Simon. She knew she looked like an idiot, but for a moment her world seemed to have clicked out of gear and she was waiting for it to change back to normal again. Simon was looking like a barrister who'd just won his case on some vital, last-minute piece of evidence, and as Caroline glanced back down at the magazines again a name came into her head: *Terence Thomas*. He was the one who'd taken these shots and he had to be the one who'd sold them to these magazines.

Caroline inspected the pictures more closely – she remembered now. Terence had popped backstage at the beauty competition to congratulate her after she'd

n and they'd done these pictures as a joke, with

Terence laughing and snapping away as Caroline giggled and did her Madonna impression, much the same as she'd been doing in the hallway this very afternoon . . .

A huge wave of anger welled up inside Caroline and, forgetting Simon was watching, she crumpled the magazines into a ball and flung them across the room. Terence Thomas . . . Caroline started to plan her revenge – that was if Geraldine Foster-Brown didn't get her hands on him first!

3
Street Life

'What about that one?'

  'Nah – too smarmy-looking.'

  'Those two?'

  'Too old.'

  'Him?'

  'His nose is running.'

  'Her, then!'

  'Too fat.'

Jeremy struck a dramatic pose and treated Caroline to what he hoped was an indignant-looking stare. 'Now look here,' he bawled, 'I have been standing in this god-forsaken street in the pouring rain for what feels like two or three hours, gawping at everyone walking past like some dirty old man, waiting while you make up your stupid mind and actually decide to interview someone. Despite the fact that two-thirds of the entire population of the universe must've passed us by during that time, you've still not seen fit to do so much as get your pen out of your bag! I was hoping by now to be back in the office with my feet on the desk, knocking back the odd cup or two of tea, but instead it looks as though we'll still be here at midnight!'

Jeremy paused for breath and a voice at his elbow chorused its agreement. 'Yeah!' chimed in a small chap with wiry red hair and dandruff. Jeremy glanced down at him and then looked back at Caroline. What was the use? When the beauty editor had suggested they do these street interviews he'd actually been stupid enough to think they sounded like fun – but that was before he'd found out he'd be working with Caroline, who spent all her time these days mooning over some drippy-sounding gink called Simon. As an added bonus he'd got Melvin to put up with, too – *Visage*'s newest hot-shot photographic assistant, and a general all-round nerd if ever he'd met one. It had been twenty minutes and two phone-calls back to the studio before Melvin had even found out how to take the lens-cap off the camera, and from then on it'd been downhill all the way.

All they had to do was to pick out a dozen flash-looking types as they cruised about down the King's Road, take a good pic, and then ask them a few crucial questions about their taste in clothes and the meaning of life, etc . . . nothing heavy, just chatty junk. Caroline, however, was treating it all as seriously as a mugging victim at a police line-up, rejecting potential targets right, left and centre for the most petty reasons. Melvin seemed happy enough – the extra time gave him a chance to find out how to put the film in his camera, but Jeremy was ready to explode.

Just as he reached blast-off, though, Caroline suddenly came to life, waving her pen and jiggling up and down. 'There! There!' she shouted. 'Those two across the road, they're perfect! Quick!'

Jeremy glanced in the direction her pen was pointing. Two very large skinheads were having an argument in the middle of the road, right outside the Great Gear Market. 'Those two?' Jeremy croaked. 'Whaddya wanna know about those two? Where they get their heads shaved? Who designs their braces?'

'Yes, yes!' Caroline squealed, missing the sarcasm in Jeremy's voice. 'Go on, ask them where they get their boots with those metal things on them from, and whether they buy their jeans faded and ready-ripped, or do it themselves! Hurry up, or they'll be gone!'

Melvin, Jeremy noticed, had already got the scent of battle in his nostrils and was bounding across the road like a lemming that's just spotted a cliff. Melvin had a major crush on Caroline though, and that, Jeremy thought, explained a lot. Melvin would've photographed the underside of a ten-ton speeding truck if Caroline had asked him to. Jeremy, however, was more interested in looking after number one.

He crossed the road with a reluctant, crawling, hands-in-pockets walk. By the time he reached the yobbos Melvin was in the thick of it like a budding Don McCullin, ducking elbows and flying fists as he clicked away madly, happily oblivious of the fact that he had at least two fingers over the lens. Jeremy reached the group just as the skinheads cottoned on that they were the subject of some media attention.

'Wassgoinon?' one of them asked. 'Waddyaplayinat?'

Jeremy tried to smile while his bladder tried to empty itself. The hulk that was towering over him did a lot to prove Darwin's theory of evolution single-handedly. 'Uh?' it persisted, closing in for the kill.

If there was one thing Jeremy had learned during his nineteen years spent as a man on the planet Earth it was this: When one male pokes another male in the shoulder with an index finger, fisticuffs are on the cards. It was written down in the ten golden commandments of manhood: 'Thou shalt not poke thy neighbour's shoulder with a stiff digit if thou wants a nose left on thy face,' right alongside other rules like: 'Spill my beer and I smack thy ear,' and: 'Thou shalt only

30

get legless if someone else is buying the rounds.' This skinhead was obviously a black belt in shoulder-poking, the way he was jabbing at Jeremy as he spoke.

Jeremy also knew the precise moment that the fight had to start, because that was also written in the rules; fists would begin to fly the exact split-second the skinhead poked him so hard that he was forced to take a step backwards. That moment had almost arrived. The first poke had been a mere glancing blow, deflected to a certain extent off the 'No Nukes' badge on Jeremy's lapel – just a warning of what was to come. The skinhead was using more force with each poke and, as hard as he tried to keep his balance, the latest one had actually made Jeremy rock on his heels. As the rubber toes of his kickers peeled reluctantly off the pavement Jeremy knew his number was up. Things seemed to move in slow motion as the two giants moved closer, slobbering over their cans of lager, and Melvin came in for the final close-up of his face. 'Something to show to the plastic surgeon,' Jeremy thought, gratefully, 'so he's got something to work on when he's remodelling my face.' Suddenly Caroline's face popped up between Jeremy and the fist that was heading his way with all the deadly accuracy of an exocet missile. 'How's it going?' she asked brightly. 'Got all the copy? Got some good snaps, Mel?'

To Jeremy's surprise the skinheads faltered, lumbering unsurely from one foot to another as Caroline beamed at them. 'Wassitallabou' ven?' one of them asked, finally.

'Oh, hasn't Jeremy told you?' Caroline wittered, giving Jeremy a disapproving look. 'We're from *Visage* magazine. We're doing some street interviews – you know, finding out what's going on in the world of real fashion, and all that! We just want to ask you a few questions about your style – like, do you wear make-up, and all your male beauty secrets, that sort of thing!' Jeremy groaned – they were all dead, now!

'*Visage*?' one of the skinheads said at last. 'Oh . . . tha's OK, we fought yew was tourists or sumffin. Goan,' he said to Melvin, posing against a wall. 'Git-mebest side!'

By the time Jeremy got back to the office that after-noon he was soggy with rain and grey with boredom. After the episode with the Neanderthal men they had all retired back to another shop doorway while Melvin tried to stop his lenses steaming up. Then Caroline had bumped into a herd of her yuppie chums from school who all spent the next two hours squealing 'OK, yah!' at one another as loudly as their lungs would allow. Even devoted Melvin caved in at that point, and gratefully fell in with Jeremy's suggestion that they call it a day and try again tomorrow.

As Jeremy staggered into reception his needs were simple – warm, dry bedding and a pint or two of brandy. Fate held other plans in store for him, though, and for the next thirty minutes or so Jeremy felt as though he had stumbled on to the set of Macbeth rather than into the offices of *Visage*.

It was well after five-thirty and the place was almost deserted apart from staff on flexi-time. The eerie whine of the Aqua-vacs echoed down the stairwells as the cleaners got to grips with the top floor of the building. Jeremy didn't mind being there alone – he often found it easier to think once all the typewriters stopped clacking and the phones stopped ringing, but Melvin, who was obviously a nerd out of working hours too, decided he couldn't go down to the studios by himself to process the film because it was so quiet down there that it gave him the creeps. He told Jeremy all this without so much as a trace of embarrassment – in fact he even seemed to imply that Jeremy would understand how he felt, and it was this that made Jeremy's blood boil the most.

'You what?' he said after Melvin's announcement. 'Gives you the creeps? Why?'

Melvin smiled an open smile and shrugged happily. 'Oh, I don't know, Jeremy – just bad vibes, or something. Come on – it won't take long. You can watch me processing!'

If Melvin's last offer had been intended as a bribe of some sort, then Jeremy could only describe himself as feeling decidedly underwhelmed. If watching Melvin processing was as exciting as watching Melvin take photographs, then Jeremy knew it would be about as riveting as watching paint dry. Melvin, however, was thrilled at the prospect of an audience and went padding off in the direction of the lift. Realizing he was lumbered, Jeremy dragged himself out of his chair and set off after the nerd, water still oozing out of the sides of his shoes as he went along.

As the two of them buzzed down the network of corridors that led to the studios, even Jeremy had to admit to himself that it was a mite creepy down there after hours. Melvin kept shushing him every time he tried to speak, and after a while he found to his disgust that he was beginning to walk along on tippy-toes. Annoyed with himself, he was just about to make Melvin jump as a joke when someone or something else did the job for him. Melvin leapt in the air, letting out a loud shriek that reverberated off every wall in

33

the building before racing back to try a full-bodied frontal attack on Jeremy's eardrums. Melvin landed on the floor as though he'd been poleaxed, and as the view cleared, Jeremy saw for the first time what had caused this impromptu display of naked terror.

A figure stood in front of them coated in wafting white robes, with the odd rotting bandage or two thrown in for good measure. It was writhing along like a sea-anemone, and the whole of its head was covered with some sort of 'Elephant-Man' white bag.

'Hi, Vanessa!' Jeremy said, tonelessly.

'Terence?' the figure asked, running white hands over Jeremy's face. Jeremy twisted the bag on Vanessa Gimlette's head around until the two slits in it were in line with her eyes.

'Jeremy!' she said. 'I thought you were Terence – I want him to run off a few shots of this special offer we're running next month.' Stepping over Melvin's prostrate form, they wound their way towards the studio.

'Special offer?' Jeremy asked.

'Yes – it's good, isn't it?' Vanessa said, taking the bag off her head and holding it out for inspection. 'It'll be a bit on the dear side, of course, but it is pure silk, and £53 is a small price to pay to stop your face getting wrinkled!'

Jeremy peered inside the bag, expecting to see some sort of massage device or something. 'How does it work?' he asked.

'Oh – you just pop it on your head before you go outside,' Vanessa said proudly. 'It protects from all those harmful rays from the sun – no rays, no wrinkles!'

What protects you from the traffic when you can't see where you're going? Jeremy wondered, but his thoughts

34

were cut off as Vanessa threw open the studio door to reveal a curious little tableau.

Terence was cowering behind one of the backdrops, trying desperately to protect his camera and other such vital pieces of equipment while Caroline set about him with a rolled-up magazine. For one split-second Jeremy and Vanessa thought of closing the door again and letting them get on with it, but curiosity got the better of them and they strolled in to watch.

Caroline paused for breath and saw them standing there. 'Look! Look!' she shouted, unrolling the magazine and poking it in front of their surprised faces. 'Look what he's done!'

Jeremy grabbed the shot of Caroline in her thong and whistled. 'Good God, Face-ache,' he said, 'you look amazing!' Vanessa tried to nudge him a warning but it was too late. Caroline rounded on him with venom.

'Amazing?' she shouted. 'You would say that! How d'you think I feel, though, knowing all those dirty old men are out there ogling my pictures! How would you feel if it was your picture in here?' Jeremy was just about to tell her, but Vanessa grabbed him firmly by the arm and led him tactfully out of the studio.

As Vanessa dragged him off up the corridor, they passed Geraldine Foster-Brown, striding along in the direction they'd just come from and, unless Jeremy were very much mistaken, wearing the same murderous look in her eyes as Caroline had just a few moments ago. Snatching a spare head-bag out of Vanessa's hands, Jeremy pulled one over his head and the pair of them tore off out of harm's way.

4

Say It With Flowers

By the time Caroline got back to her flat that evening the manic gleam was beginning to die down in her eyes. Clutched in one hand she had the evidence she needed to prove to snotty Simon just who had integrity and who didn't.

Glowing with victory, she re-read the two page statement she had forced Terence into writing, informing 'whom it may concern' that the bikini shots had been published in the various magazines without Caroline's knowledge, and that their publication in no way implied that this was now Caroline's newest career venture, despite captions to the contrary. Terence had signed the statement at the bottom of each page, and there were also signatures from two reliable, responsible witnesses alongside them. Squirming with glee, she ripped a page out of her shorthand notebook and added a sarcastic little note of her own before packaging the whole lot up and sliding it through Simon's letterbox.

Expecting some sort of answering broadside, Caroline paced about her flat for the entire weekend before writing off Simon and his scruples and his integrity as a complete dead loss.

'He's just a stupid intellectual snob!' she announced, whirling the sticky corner of an apricot Danish round in the chocolaty froth on top of her coffee.

Jeremy peered around the coffee bar to see who she might be talking about. Yet another session of street interviews had been rained off all morning, but this time Jeremy didn't mind so much. Chelsea were playing a 'friendly' at home, and he didn't fancy waylaying a wandering band of marauders from the Intercity Firm just to ask them what colour mascara they were wearing. Not without a riot shield and the odd can of CS gas tucked under his braces, anyway.

Besides, the *Il Carramba Cappuccino Bar* made quite a neat little refuge, considering. The coffee machine hissed and gurgled away throatily, happily drowning out Jimmy Young's patter on the radio, condensation trickled down the windows, and the steam rose from diners' wet clothing just as gustily as it came off the plates of spaghetti and lasagne the waitresses were throwing around from table to table. Caroline was subdued and thoughtful and Melvin had shut up rabbiting and found out how to work his camera at last. *All's well with the world!* Jeremy thought, ladling the parmesan into his minestrone and making patterns on top with the black pepper. Then Caroline started her outburst and he groaned inwardly.

'I don't know what I ever saw in him in the first place!' she said, bottom lip quivering like a mound of zabaglione. 'He's not even that good-looking – really!'

Jeremy stopped inspecting the other punters and put down his spoon with a sigh. Simple Simon again, that drongo! 'He's a right gink,' he agreed, nodding wisely. 'And anyway, he's too old for you.'

Caroline's eyes blazed. 'Too old?' she wavered. 'No he's not – he's only in his early twenties!'

'He's a Hooray Henry – a chinless wonder, probably has All-Bran for breakfast!' Jeremy went on, warming to his theme.

'No, he's not!' Caroline snorted, rising up in her

chair and making Melvin's camera fly to the floor with a loud clatter. Melvin coughed nervously and sank under the table to survey the damage. They could hear him piecing bits together and his bum made a large bulge in the red checked tablecloth.

'I·bet he dabs Dettol on his pimples and uses Aramis to drown the smell . . .' Jeremy shouted, treading on some unrecognizable but obviously vital part of Melvin's anatomy as he leant forward across the table. 'I know the type, Caroline – so short and stunted they can barely see over the wheel of their flamin' Range Rovers. I bet he wears green wellies *and* keeps them on in bed. C'mon Caroline, admit it – the guy's a prize pratt!'

'You've never even seen Simon!' Caroline squealed. 'He's tall and slim, not stunted, and he wears Imperial Leather, and anyway, you think everyone's a pratt, everyone you meet!'

'No I don't!' Jeremy said.

'Yes you do!' Caroline yelled.

'Don't!' Jeremy repeated. 'Name one other then, go on!'

'Melvin, for one!' Caroline stormed. 'You're always calling him a pratt!' There was a small squeal from under the tablecloth but Caroline and Jeremy only had ears for each other.

'Too easy!' Jeremy announced. 'Name another!'

'Oh, anyone, everyone!' Caroline said, waving her arms in the air. 'You tell me one person you don't think is a pratt.'

Jeremy paused and gave the question serious thought. 'I don't think you're a pratt,' he said, quietly. There was a brief pause and the whole coffee bar fell silent. Italians are very good at sensing a potentially romantic situation, and waiters stood in silent attention while waitresses bustled closer to beam encouragement. The cappuccino machine settled down to a quiet, simpering hum and even Jimmy Young put a Julio Englesias on his turntable. Caroline stood in frozen animation, mouth agape like a stuffed trout in a display case.

Jeremy cleared his throat and twitched nervously, not quite sure what he'd said wrong. Caroline was looking at him strangely, and he was not sure it was a look he liked. He preferred her angry – her eyes had gone all gooey now and she looked like a drip.

'That's the nicest compliment you've ever paid me, Jeremy,' she said, gawping.

'I . . . I . . . it is?' Jeremy stammered, looking nervously at his audience for the next cue. The waitresses nodded and giggled, egging him on to better things. 'Well, I'm one compliment up on you then, Caro – you never pay me any!'

Caroline smiled bashfully, studying Jeremy's face as though she were seeing him for the first time in her life. 'You've got nice eyelashes,' she whispered, eventually. The audience murmured their approval.

'Nice?' Jeremy asked, smiling. 'Surely *nice* is a pretty lame word for a budding writer to be using?'

'They're lovely, then,' Caroline said. 'All long and glossy, like spider's legs.'

Jeremy could feel himself blushing. He could also see his minestrone getting cold and he wondered how he could call this whole caboodle off as soon as possible.

He wasn't going to get away that lightly, though. The audience had sat patiently through the first act and now they wanted some real drama for their money.

This was nitty-gritty time, when real men stood up to be counted and pratts like Simon chickened out. Jeremy took a deep breath and reached in his pocket for a cigarette before remembering he didn't smoke.

'Caroline,' he began, realizing to his horror that her eyes were getting even gooeyer, 'You . . . you . . . you've got smashing skin. It's all . . . all pink . . . and . . . and . . . freckled, like . . . like . . .' Jeremy looked around for inspiration and his eyes lighted on the menu on the wall, 'Like . . . a slice of corned beef!' he finished, inspired and relieved. A small wince of pain flickered across Caroline's face, but the audience were ecstatic. This boy was a true romantic! Jeremy intensified his attack.

'You shouldn't be wasting yourself on Simon,' he said, softly, 'you're too good for him. If he truly thought anything of you, he'd like you whether you were blonde, brunette, or bald. It's you that counts, not the way you're dolled up.'

It was at this point that the stooge took the stage. Melvin had managed to piece his precious camera together ages ago, and had been playing possum under the table while he waited for what he thought sounded like a tactful moment to emerge. He hadn't been expecting the entire balcony scene from *Romeo and Juliet* though, and an acute and sudden attack of cramp in the right calf took the problem of tactful timing out of his hands. The entire table, including cold mine-strone and half-dunked Danish pastries, suddenly rose up in the air as Melvin got his first spasm of pain. Thinking they were witnessing some sort of spiritual intervention, the audience oohed and ahhed, but once they saw it was only Melvin with cramp the spell was broken. Within minutes the coffee bar was back to its usual bustling indifference and Caroline was left to blot coffee off her trousers while Jeremy was promptly served with the bill by a very disappointed waiter.

The fresh air outside had an instantly-sobering effect on Jeremy and panic started to set in. *Fancy Caroline?* he thought to himself, *you must need a holiday, mate – or a brain transplant! Why, even young Melvin would probably be more fun on an evening out!* Jeremy laughed out loud as he imagined the expressions on his mates' faces if he strolled into the King's Head or The Camden Palace with Caroline on one arm. Then he took another sidelong glance at her, waiting patiently for another victim for one of her interviews, and the thought crossed his mind that his mates just might be jealous.

He watched Caroline as she pottered across the busy main road, Melvin in tow, to stop a particularly horsey-looking girl on the other side, and he found himself worrying about her getting run over. He also found himself admiring the colour of her hair as a pale shaft of sunlight filtered through the clouds, and it was at that point Jeremy knew he had to be cracking up.

It had to be the strain of the job, he told himself – competing with Caro and Seraphina these past few weeks was obviously taking its toll. Caroline was a friend, that was all. He wouldn't be seen dead taking out someone who dressed like that – his street cred. would be right out the window! Then he tried to remember how long it'd been since he'd asked anyone out and, solution in sight, he set off to scour the landscape for some proper talent.

As it turned out, Jeremy didn't have to scour very far. As he bounded into reception that afternoon he was forced to brake so hard his shoes left scorch-marks on the carpet. For one blissful moment he thought some genie somewhere had been listening and decided to grant his wish. Waiting expectantly in front of his eyes were at least three settees-full of the most stunning girls he'd ever seen in his life. Looking over at the receptionist for an explanation, he saw the desk was empty and assumed she'd gone on one of her sixteen-million trips a day to the loo. He looked back at the girls again.

'Hi!' he said, smiling broadly. 'I'm Jeremy – I work here at *Visage*. Can I be of any . . . er. . . assistance?' A couple of the girls smiled politely and the rest just stared.

'We're here for the interview,' one of them said eventually, unfolding a pair of the longest tanned legs Jeremy could ever remember seeing in his life.

'For the fashion spread,' another one added, pouting at herself in the mirror she was holding.

Jeremy gulped. 'Oh, for sure,' he said, trying to sound more confident than he felt, 'the next fashion feature. Well, that's my department, actually, so you're in luck. I just passed by at the right time.'

'You're in charge of the bookings?' one of the models asked him, raising one eyebrow and looking him up and down carefully.

'Well . . . er . . . yes, you could say that,' Jeremy said, sitting down on an empty lounger. 'And are these your portfolios?' he asked, grabbing a couple of black leather folders off the table in front of him.

'My agency told me I'd be interviewed by some-one called Geraldine Foster-Brown,' one of the girls said, running one hand through her mane of tousled, chestnut-coloured hair.

'Oh, yes . . . yes, you will,' Jeremy said, flicking

wildly through her photographs, 'but I suppose the final decision will be left up to me – as usual! Geraldine sort of organizes these castings for me. She's what you might describe as the liaison officer around here – she does all the hard work and I just drift in at the final stages!' The girls all looked round at one another and a couple of them shrugged. Jeremy buried his head in the next portfolio.

'Bébé?' he asked, looking at the name on the cover. 'Bébé what?'

'Just Bébé,' the girl with the pout told him in a strong Southern American drawl. 'Ah just use the one name for ma job.'

'Oh, you're American, eh?' Jeremy said, listening to himself and deciding he'd just won the competition to find the pratt of the year hands down. Now he knew how Melvin must feel all the time, and the thought made him shudder.

'All three of us are,' the leggy girl told him, stretching herself out even further on the settee. 'We came over together for the shows. Ah'm Cherie and this here's Desirée.' The girl who was sitting next to her and was dressed like a cheerleader grinned politely and leaned forward to shake Jeremy's hand. All the other models in reception seemed to have gone back to their books and magazines, so Jeremy decided to press on with these three.

'And what agency are you with?' he asked, trying to sound knowledgeable.

'Wall, we're here for a month an' we've booked in with "The Model Shop", but in the US we're all with "Kitty's Kits",' Desirée told him. 'They're really tops out there – d'you know of them?'

'Sure, sure!' Jeremy said, lying. 'Fantastic, fantastic.'

43

Suddenly he sprang to his feet so quickly that the three girls jumped. Geraldine Foster-Brown had just been sighted turning the corner on her way into reception.

'Well, that's all fine, then . . .' Jeremy said, backing away quickly. 'We'll . . . we'll let the agency know . . .'

'Do we get the job?' Bébé asked.

'Oh . . . yes . . . I should think so . . .' Jeremy stammered.

'But what about the other girls?' Cherie said, looking around in astonishment. 'Aren't you even going to look at their books?' – but Jeremy had gone, flying off down the corridor, still sweating from the close shave he'd just had.

Once inside the office he slammed the door and sank into a chair. 'Never again,' he swore to himself. 'The old ticker can't stand it. Next time you want to find yourself a girlfriend you can do it on home ground like The King's Head, and leave the studio chat-ups to professionals like Terence Thomas!' And shoving thoughts of girls like Bébé, Desirée and even Caroline firmly to the back of his mind, Jeremy picked up his notebook and got down to some work at last.

Caroline arrived home that evening in a state of total confusion. First there had been the strange scene in the coffee bar with Jeremy, and then other people at work had started acting oddly towards her, too.

She'd been quietly helping herself to a burnt hand and a beaker of tea from the vending machine in the corridor when Terence had rushed up and patted her on the head. 'Well done, Carrots,' he'd beamed. 'I know we've had our little differences of opinion, but I always knew you had it in you! Bet Jeremy and Seraphina won't be so pleased when they see it, though – they'll have to pull their socks up if they want that job now!' And he'd shot off again before she'd had a chance to ask him what he was babbling on about.

Geraldine Foster-Brown was the other puzzle. She'd never gone out of her way to be pleasant to Caroline, but then again, she was competing with Geraldine's daughter for the job at *Visage*. The look she'd given Caroline that afternoon, though, was one of pure hatred – in fact Caroline still shuddered when she thought of it. She couldn't understand what she'd done wrong – or right, come to that.

As she walked into the hallway of her block of flats though, all her thoughts about Jeremy and Geraldine were pushed right out of her head. Lying on top of the mailboxes, over her box in particular, was the most gorgeous, enormous, expensive-looking bouquet of flowers Caroline had ever seen. She walked over towards it and peered at it for a long time, standing on tiptoe, before she slid open the small envelope that was attached to one corner and read the note that was inside.

'*Please forgive me,*' it read. '*I was wrong and I was very rude. I love you. Simon.*'

Caroline's knees buckled as the strength seemed to drain out of her body. In one sudden rush she knew that all the awful things she'd said about Simon, and all the decisions she'd made to forget him were rubbish – he was handsome and he was perfect, and she loved him too.

Lifting the flowers gingerly from the boxes, she gazed at each one through the sellophane, trying to memorize them for future reference. 'Your father

45

bought me these flowers,' she would tell their children in the decades to come. 'It changed the whole nature of our relationship. Up until the moment I received the . . .' Caroline studied the flowers again, '. . . the roses and freesias and beautiful pale pink orchids, I was almost considering going off with a young rake called Jeremy, but in the nick of time . . .'

Caroline's thoughts were interrupted by the sound of footsteps in the hallway behind her. She spun round quickly and then caught her breath as she saw Simon standing there, waiting. Holding the bouquet out in her arms, she tried to speak but her voice broke. 'Simon!' she managed at last. 'So you did get my note explaining everything! Of course I forgive . . .' But before she could finish, a taxi door banged loudly in the street outside and another set of footsteps pattered into the hall behind them.

'Your note?' Simon asked, but it was too late to answer. A tall, beautiful, elegant-looking girl with eyes the colour of smoke and long, silvery-blonde hair swept up, snaking her arm into the crook of Simon's elbow. Oblivious to the embarrassed silence all around her, she stared first at Simon, then at Caroline, and lastly at the flowers. Finally the penny dropped and a look of total surprise crossed her lovely face.

'Simon!' she shouted. 'Oh my God, why didn't you tell me? How could you be so secretive?' Her hands flew up to her mouth and Caroline prepared herself for a scene of the highest order. The girl would obviously be upset, but when she realized Simon was in love with Caroline, she would have to understand and go off and get knotted.

The girl looked at Simon's face as though expecting an explanation but Simon had turned to stone. Finally she walked towards Caroline, who flinched, expecting a slap round the face. To Caroline's horror, though, the girl appeared to be smiling happily when she reached her. Before Caroline could move, she scooped the flowers out of her arms and held them up to her own face, inhaling the perfume deeply as she did so.

'Oh!' she exclaimed. 'They're beautiful! Thank you so much darling,' and she kissed Simon full on the mouth. Pulling him off towards the lift, she suddenly turned back to Caroline. 'And you got this nice young lady from Interflora to wait with them, too!' she said, smiling patronizingly. 'I'm sorry, dear – I should've thanked you properly.' Fishing in her bag she finally pulled out a 50p piece and pressed it into Caroline's hand. 'Thank you so much!' she said happily, then the lift doors closed and they were out of sight at last.

Caroline didn't think she would hold on that long. Sinking down on to the bottom step, she sunk her head into her hands and sobbed.

5
By Royal Command

'Well, I suppose it's better than a poke in the eye with
a blunt stick,' Jeremy said, peering hard into Geraldine
Foster-Brown's magnifying make-up mirror and having
an eyeball-to eyeball confrontation with a large, mean-
looking blackhead that seemed to have taken up permanent residence in the greasy crease of his left nostril.
Pushing the end of his nose over at a ninety-degree
angle and pursing his lips hard, Jeremy decided the
one solitary blemish on his otherwise-perfect features
would need to be compulsorily re-housed – it was
spoiling the view. 'Go and find accommodation on
Melvin's nose,' he told it. 'I'm sure he could find a
nice cosy little nook for you somewhere!'

Terence Thomas looked away quickly. His stomach
was still heaving from the mushroom and beancurd
stew that Seraphina had cooked for him the night
before, and he had no desire to study Jeremy's ado-
lescent zits in full glorious technicolour.

'I thought you'd be chuffed, mate!' Terence said,
flicking through Geraldine's private diary and trying to
analyse all the squiggles and scribble that filled the
pages. 'Chance of a trip to sunny Scotland, well away
from all those street interviews you're always griping
about? Booze and birds all on expenses? Wassamatter
Jerry – had a sex change or something?'

Jeremy pondered over the question for a long time.
What *was* wrong? He *had* been getting cheesed off
with standing in the pouring rain in the King's Road

every day and Terry had just offered him the chance to make good and prove his worth on this shoot he was doing up in Scotland. Just being the run-around might not've sounded like too much of a job, but if he could help with the locations and do a bit of styling on set . . .

Suddenly, for no real reason that he could see, Caroline's face popped up in Jeremy's head and refused to go away. With a feeling of panic, he realized that he'd miss working with her – miss being with her, come to that. The magnifying mirror dropped out of his hand with a clatter. 'I'll go!' he shouted, firmly. 'It'll be great. Thanks Terry, me old chum!'

The trip would squash this stupid infatuation with old carrot-tops in no time, Jeremy thought. What was it Terry'd just said? – *'booze and birds on expenses'*? Jeremy suddenly felt a gnawing worry in the pit of his stomach.

'What was it you said about birds, Terry?' he asked, trying to sound nonchalant.

'Yeah!' Terry told him, grinning. 'You'll have your pick, devastating young Adonis like yourself! And as I'm spoken for,' he went on, nodding towards Seraphina's empty desk, 'you've got no competition, either. They can fight for your favours between the three of them!'

Jeremy suddenly started to feel very sick. 'Three of them?' he asked, nervously.

'Oh yes,' Terence said, leering. 'Didn't I tell you – we've got three lovely models going along, too. They're doing the fashion spread for us, and a more eye-boggling little trio you couldn't ask to meet! Legs, Lips and Lusciousness I call 'em – they'll be right up your street, no problem!'

'And . . . er . . . what are their real names?' Jeremy asked, trying to adopt a manly grin, despite the fact that his knees were quaking.

'Real names?' Terence asked, raising his eyebrows in mock surprise. 'Oh, well, let me see . . . they're a bit daft, actually, but don't let the names put you off . . . something like Bébé, Cherie, and Desirée, I think, but you'll soon forget the names when you get to inspect the goods! But hang on, Jerry,' Terence added, trying hard not to laugh at Jeremy's white face in front of him, 'you already know them, don't you?'

Jeremy thought he might pass out.

'When I mentioned your name they all got quite excited,' Terence went on. 'I got quite jealous, in fact! They all reckoned they couldn't wait to see you again to thank you properly for getting them the job in the first place. I couldn't understand what they were on about – I told them they must've got you muddled up with someone else 'cos you were only the junior run-around, but they described you to a tee!'

Jeremy's eyes were like saucers. 'Wh . . . wh . . . what did they say when you t . . . tt . . . told them that?' he asked.

'What – that you were only the office junior?' Terence asked, getting up to leave before he exploded altogether. 'Well . . . not a lot, really. In fact they went quite quiet, as I recall. Still, I shouldn't let it worry you, mate. You'll have enough time alone with them on those misty hillsides to persuade them you've got other resources than a good job – won't you?' and Terence stormed out of the office, slamming the door shut quickly behind him. One more look at Jeremy's horror-struck little face and he knew he was going to crease up altogether!

In fact, the models had told him exactly what'd happened at the interview and he'd agreed to help them with their wind-up. Jeremy was going to be mincemeat once those three got their hands on him, and Terence had to admit that he deserved all he got. Somehow he was beginning to look forward to this trip. At first he'd thought it was just going to be damp and depressing, leaving Seraphina behind and wandering around in all those mists and marshes, and when he'd met those three American Cupie-dolls Geraldine'd chosen to do the modelling, his heart had sunk to his boots. Now he could feel his spirits lifting, though. Seraphina would be safely tucked away covering the Italian fashion shows under the eagle-eye care of her mother, and this little affair with Jeremy looked like being fun. Swinging his tripod over his shoulder, Terence set off towards the studio, whistling happily.

'D'you want the good news or the bad news?' Seraphina asked Caroline as she bounced into the office, blonde hair gleaming. One look at her friend's pale face and red-rimmed eyes, though, and Seraphina realized she'd better save the bad news till last – Caroline looked as though she'd had more than her fair share of it already!

'Look!' she announced, waving two tickets under Caroline's nose. 'These came through the post this morning – two tickets to go to the exclusive press ball at the opening night of the "Nightlite" club in Shaftesbury Avenue. Terry and I can't go because I'll be in Italy by then, so I thought you might like them. There'll be loads of celebrities there – rock stars and everything! You'll have a great time!'

Caroline tried to smile.

51

'I *thought*,' Seraphina went on, sitting down and dropping her voice a few decibels, 'well, I thought maybe you could use the other ticket to invite that guy Simon you're always on about – it would be the perfect excuse to ask him out, wouldn't it? He couldn't say no, could he, and then you could turn up looking even more devastating than usual and set about seducing him under the laser beams!'

'Th . . . thanks, Seraphina,' Caroline said, taking the tickets and pulling a fresh tissue out of her drawer to dab at her sniffling pink nose. 'And what was that about the bad news?'

Seraphina looked doubtful. She hadn't exactly been expecting Caroline to throw herself at her feet with gratitude, but she would've liked a quick glimmer of pleasure out of her at least as she gave her the tickets – after all, it wasn't every day you got the chance to go to an exclusive do like that! If Caroline was still looking miserable, it had to be something serious, and Seraphina wasn't sure she should be giving her the next piece of news in that case.

'You were late in this morning, Caroline,' she said, seriously. 'I think Dottie's on the warpath – she's been looking everywhere for you, and she told me to tell you she wants to see you as soon as you get in!'

Caroline looked tired. 'Oh God – so that's it then,' she said, fiddling with her hankie and keeping her head down. 'I must've lost the job as well. Congratulations, Seraphina – it looks like you've got the full-time fixture. I can't see Jeremy being offered the job after all those dreary street interviews got rained off!'

'I'm sorry, Caro,' Seraphina began. 'I know I always wanted to get the job, but I didn't want you to fall out of the running just because you were late for work

52

once – why, I must've been late nearly every other morn . . .' but Geraldine had overheard her daughter's confession being blurted out, and she yelled at her from behind the office partition.

'Seraphina!' she shouted, cutting her daughter off in mid-sentence. 'Come in here. I want you to help me arrange our flight-times for tomorrow. I can't seem to be able to get booked on a plane to Rome unless we go second class! Caroline,' she added, 'stop snivelling and get in to see Dottie – I'm getting fed up with the sight of all your soggy tissues lying around this office!'

Seraphina shrugged in embarrassment and tried to smile encouragement at Caroline, but the girl made a small choking sound and shot off down the corridor to see the editor and to hear her fate.

Dottie's door was open and Caroline peered into the office to see the editor sitting back in her seat with her feet up on the desk, in the middle of what was obviously a rather heavy telephone conversation. She waved her arms angrily, ignoring Caroline altogether as she yelled into the mouthpiece.

'You're talking figures to me again, Bernard!' she bawled. 'I don't see the point! *Visage* is an institution – we are the word of fashion in this country. No one should be able to dictate to us – we're the leader!' Suddenly she spotted Caroline and her tone changed. 'Look – I'll have to get back to you on this,' she said, turning her chair around and waving Caroline into a seat opposite. 'I'm busy right now and I need time to think things over,' and she slammed the receiver down noisily, making Caroline jump.

'Caroline?' Dottie asked, waiting for an identifying nod before she went on. 'You were late this morning – I was looking for you!'

Caroline paused. She realized she ought to explain why she'd missed her train, but the story of her upset with Simon and how she'd lain awake all night crying, was too upsetting and long-winded for her to launch into. And besides, Dottie would think she was an idiot if she told her about the incident with the flowers. At the same time, though, she didn't want to make up a lie . . .

Fortunately, Dottie solved the problem by butting in before Caroline had a chance to explain. 'I wanted to congratulate you,' she said, beaming.

Caroline jumped just as hard as she had when the phone was slammed down. Congratulate her? For what? Being a prime example of whining, unliberated womanhood? Had they decided to give her the Wally-Woman-of-the-Year award or something?

'Wonderful, wonderful!' Dottie went on. 'How did you manage it? Super photos, too! That little chap Melvin must be improving at last.'

Caroline rubbed her eyes in disbelief. What *could* Dottie be going on about?

The editor picked some sheets of paper off her desk and read through them, smiling. Focusing her tear-blurred eyes at last, Caroline recognized one of her street interviews. But surely that couldn't be what all the fuss was about?

'I was hoping you could pad it out a bit more, Caroline,' Dottie told her, holding the interview out for her to see. 'I want to turn it into a double-page spread, especially with these illustrations. Could you add a bit more, d'you think? Describe her more fully, go through her outfit in more detail, that sort of thing? I know you must've been rushed at the time, but anything else you can think of will do – what her voice

54

sounded like, how old she looked, all that sort of thing!'

Caroline read the interview in stunned silence – it was the one she'd done with a rather horsey-looking Sloane Ranger, just after the strange scene with Jeremy in the coffee bar. The interview had been so boring that Caroline had almost scrubbed it altogether, but some of Melvin's other photos that day had been a disaster, and she'd been forced to keep it in. Perhaps dropping Melvin's camera on the floor had done it good, because these photos were some of the best he'd ever taken. *Still,* Caroline thought, *I don't see they merit this amount of fuss!*

The girl in the photos was quite attractive, but she wasn't what anyone would describe as fashionable, especially with that awful headscarf knotted tightly under her chin! Funnily enough though, as Caroline inspected the pictures properly for the first time, the girl's face looked almost familiar for some reason . . .

'She wouldn't give a Christian name,' Caroline told Dottie, rather embarrassed by the fact that she'd had to put the girl down as 'Miss Windsor', when all the other interviews were done on first-name terms.

'Well, she always did have a good sense of humour,' Dottie said, chuckling. 'But surely you didn't ask her name? She must've had a good laugh about that when she got back to the Palace!'

Caroline gulped. Had she heard Dottie right? Then she picked up the photo again and her hand flew up to her mouth.

'This is a real exclusive,' Dottie went on, happily. 'Just to walk up to royalty in the street like that and have the sheer cheek to get an interview! I love the sort of bold questions you asked her, too! "*What colour mascara do you use?"* – brilliant! *"How many pairs of tights do you get through in a week?"* – wonderful! *"Who do you like best – Boy George or George Michael?"* – inspired! Much more interesting than the usual stuff they get asked about horse trials and inner-city pollution! Look – ' Dottie finished, rising to her feet and shoving the interview and the rest of the photos across the desk at Caroline, 'tidy this lot up, pad it out a bit like I said, and we'll try to get it in the next issue. Oh,' she added, stopping Caroline as she shuffled out of the door, still shellshocked, 'and you might tell Melvin one of those pictures *could* be on the cover if we get the OK from design and layout. That should keep him happy for a while!' And Dottie picked up her phone to get back to the row she was having as Caroline walked in.

Caroline stepped outside Dottie's office and walked straight into Melvin, who had heard his name mentioned inside and who had been listening unsuccessfully at the door for the last five minutes. The interview and the photos flew everywhere and they both dived to the floor in the scramble to pick them up.

'Rejected again, I suppose?' Melvin asked, inspecting his photos as he arranged them into a tidy pile. 'What was it this time? I thought these ones looked OK. Was Dottie very annoyed? Maybe if I tried that new filter out next time, to diffuse some of that strong sunlight . . .' But as Melvin looked up at Caroline he found to his absolute surprise and amazement that she was smiling broadly at him.

'Melvin!' she shouted, flinging her arms round him and jumping up and down. 'Oh . . . I could kiss you!' and she planted a huge smacker on his startled cheek. 'You don't know what we did, either, do you?' she asked, seeing the look of shock on Melvin's little face. 'No wonder everyone's been congratulating me all week – and here I was thinking I was going in to get the sack! Melvin, this is the kind of scoop other writers dream about, and we didn't even realize what we'd done! Look – look at this picture again,' Caroline said, holding up the biggest close-up for Melvin's inspection, 'and then imagine the face with a tiara on top of it instead of a headscarf! Oh, Melvin, we're so lucky – this might even get on the cover next month!'

As the penny dropped and Melvin began to blush with pride and shock at their cheek, Caroline had another thought and started fishing for something in her pocket. 'By the way, Melvin,' she said, pulling out two small pieces of paper and smoothing them carefully, 'I just happen to've been given these two tickets for a press party at the new "Nightlite" club and, seeing how we make such a good team, I wondered whether – if you're not doing anything on that particular evening . . . ?'

Melvin nearly exploded with ecstasy – first an interview with a princess, then the chance of a cover shot, and now a date with Caroline! *Surely*, he thought, as he made his dazed way back to the darkroom, *this is more pleasure than a man could stand in an entire lifetime, let alone in the space of a few mere minutes . . .*

6

Spaghetti With Meatballs

'What's up dear?' Geraldine Foster-Brown asked her daughter as she hoovered up another mouthful of Spaghetti Bolognese, whipping a small pair of sharp nail scissors out of her bag to slice off any rogue strands of pasta that still dangled helplessly out of her lips after all her sucking power had been used up. Dabbing at the small traces of brown sauce that had started to congeal, like freckles, on her chin, Geraldine peered hard at Seraphina and frowned. Was her daughter beginning to look gaunt? Could she possibly be pining, or did her eyes deceive her?

Seraphina put down her fork and sighed. 'Oh, I don't know,' she said, looking even more beautiful than normal. 'I suppose it's just that this is all so . . . so . . . Italian, really.'

'But we are in Italy, dear,' Geraldine reminded her daughter. 'What the hell did you expect? Beefeaters and Yorkshire pudding?' and she sipped noisily from a glass of ice-cold Soave.

'No, not really,' Seraphina explained. 'It's just that this is the fourth fashion show in a row where they've served free 'Press-only' Spaghetti Bolognese while Luciano Pavarotti warbles "*O Sole Mio*" on some tape in the background!'

'We had pizza at the last show, not spaghetti,' Geraldine corrected her. 'And anyway, if you don't like the food and the music, the least you could try

58

and do is to pay attention to some of the clothes! The Italians are beautiful designers!'

'But when you phoned Dottie last night I heard you telling her the stuff over here was awful this season!' Seraphina wailed.

'That is another matter,' Geraldine snapped. 'I was just trying to be patriotic – how would it look if I rushed back to London raving about a load of foreign merchandise? The British market would collapse within the week!'

'So why do we have to trail round this circuit of shows, then,' Seraphina asked, 'if you're not going to write anything about them anyway?'

Geraldine looked at her daughter as though she'd just lost all of her marbles. 'Why?' she asked. 'Why?'

Seraphina nodded. 'Yes – and why drag me all the way out here to follow you about instead of letting me start on that "Workclothes" feature I wanted to do with Terence?'

Geraldine felt herself shudder at the mere mention of the photographer's name, but then she remembered her little plan and sat back in her chair to relax. Packing 'Medallion Man' off to Scotland with a carload of bubblegum-popping sexbombs had been an inspired idea – a few days locked away with that lot and he'd forget Seraphina even existed. Geraldine had hand-picked the three girls herself at the casting – one leggy girl, one with a huge, sexy, pouting mouth, and one that had a cleavage you could post mail in. Geraldine knew Terry's taste in women of old, and she knew that he'd never be able to keep his sweaty hands off those three!

Now Geraldine had other fish to fry. Turning Terence off was one thing, but if her daughter was left pining all over the place she'd never get it together to steal the job at *Visage* away from Caroline and Jeremy. Geraldine had to get her daughter motivated again, and she thought she knew just the way to do it, too . . .

Terence watched Jeremy with amusement as they waited for their flight to be called. He'd been to the loo so many times that the attendant was thinking of getting a revolving door fitted for him, and now he was hopping from one foot to another, whistling under his breath while his eyes darted about like jumping beans.

'Get a grip, mate!' Terence laughed, slapping Jeremy hard between the shoulderblades and nearly making him jump out of his clothes. 'You'll never get through the security check, jumping around all sweaty like that! They'll think you're carrying a bagful of bombs or something!'

Jeremy paled visibly as Terence studied his watch. 'Those girls are late,' he announced, chuckling. 'But I suppose that's the women's prerogative. What's up with you, anyway, Jerry?' he asked, turning back to his pasty-faced assistant. 'You look like you've just spotted the pilot reeling out the boozer with a joint between his lips – you nervous of flying, or what?'

Jeremy nodded, glad to have an excuse for his fear. 'Yeah,' he told Terence, smiling and trying to look sheepish, 'it's my first flight and I never could see what it is that holds those flamin' great monsters up in the air!'

'Don't worry,' Terence told him. 'The flight to Scotland'll be over so quickly you won't have time to take your seatbelt off, and anyway,' he added, waving suddenly and smiling with relief, 'I'm sure the girls will volunteer to hold your hand and look after you until touchdown – look, here they come!'

As Jeremy scoured the terminus desperately, looking for a place to hide, the crowded area suddenly parted like the Red Sea as the shrieking, whooping trio of girls made their way across to them. In a wild state of ecstatic over-excitement, they leapt and jumped, careering into each other and into any other passengers who happened to get too close, swinging enormous Gucci travel bags above their heads like cheerleader pom-poms and leaving a trail of destruction like a bull elephant on the rampage.

'Hey, wowee, yowzah! Tereeeee! Wow! Yeah!' they went, drowning out vital passenger information from the intercom. 'Here! We're here! Hey, hey, waddya say? Tereeee! Jereeee! Wow!' The whistles, yelps and shouts went on well after the girls had collapsed in a breathless heap at their feet, and for at least ten minutes it would only take the slightest reaction from Terence, like a sardonic: 'Hi, girls!' to make them break out in another flurry of whoops.

The strange thing as far as Jeremy was concerned, though, was the fact that his body as yet seemed to still be intact. By now he'd expected his intestines to be dangling from the ceiling like paper chains while other vital organs were being scooped up from the floor and being earmarked for potential transplants – why, he'd even brought his kidney donor card, just in case it came in handy. So far, though, he hadn't received so much as a black look from the models, let alone a killer karate chop. In fact, he had to admit, they were doing their best to look friendly!

As their flight was called Jeremy received an even

bigger shock. Cherie sidled up as he went to collect his battered sportsbag and snatched it out of his hand. 'Allow me!' she whispered, licking her already lip-glossed-lips and pouting provocatively. 'Carrying your bag is the least I can do, Jerry – under the circumstances!'

Jeremy blushed. 'Oh . . . er . . . ta!' he mumbled, ambling off towards the departure gate.

'No – I want to carry Jerry's bag!' Bébé suddenly shouted, grabbing at one handle and pushing Cherie roughly out of the way.

'Hey, me!' Desirée yelled, joining the tussle and elbowing the other two. 'Me too! I want to show him how grateful I am he got us this job! Give it to me!'

Suddenly both handles ripped off the bag and it went flying across the lounge like a football heading for the goal. A passing dog decided to race Jeremy for the privilege of reaching it first, and unfortunately for Jeremy, the dog won. Grabbing it firmly between his teeth, growling from deep in his gullet, the dog made it clear that he was ready for a game. As Jeremy dived towards it, arms akimbo, the dog shot off like a greyhound, eyes rolling with pleasure as he went. As the girls squealed encouragement, Jeremy took up the chase, only managing to stop the charade with a flying rugby tackle over three large suitcases and one very small child. Clutching the handleless, dribble-covered bag firmly under one arm, he silently joined the queue and boarded what fortunately turned out to be the right plane.

To his horror, as he walked down the aisle he saw Cherie waving and patting the empty seat next to her, while Bébé and Desirée jiggled about in the seats behind. As it appeared to be the only empty seat on the plane, Jeremy sank into it gingerly, barely hearing the overdone apologies from the models as they fastened his seatbelt, adjusted his pillow, and read his safety instructions out loud to him.

'Hey, Jerreee,' Desirée cooed as Cherie reclined his seat, 'we were so proud of the way you tackled that lil' ol' doggie! Wow, you can really run! Do you do a lot of sport – are you really fit?'

Jeremy looked worried. There was something about the way Desirée had looked at him as she said the words 'Sport' and 'Fit' that made him suspect she had more in mind than a quick game of ping-pong.

'Look! Look!' Bébé suddenly squealed. 'Look what we got for you, Jerry – to say thank you for getting us this job!'

There was a loud bang in Jeremy's ear and for one moment he thought that he'd been shot. Then he opened his eyes to see a smiling stewardess pouring glasses of champagne from a magnum-sized bottle. Staring at the bubbles as they rose in his glass, and gazing round at the girls' grateful faces, Jeremy felt totally confused. Surely Terence said he'd told them the truth about his job? If they knew he'd been trying it on, then why were they being so nice to him? Then he saw Terence wink at him from across the aisle and the penny dropped – the photographer had been joking! Of course he hadn't let on that Jeremy was only the junior – he was just pulling Jeremy's leg to get him worried! Well that little wind-up had worked good and proper, Jeremy thought, grinning at Terence to let him know he was sussed.

With a deep sigh of relief, Jeremy took a long slug of champagne and lay back in his seat to enjoy the rest of his flight. After the sixth glass the lovely faces of

63

Bébé, Cherie and Desirée were beginning to swim in front of his eyes, and he leant his head back to catch up on his sleep . . .

Turning the waiter away after the third offer of a glass of Chianti, Seraphina looked at her watch and hoped that Terence's flight was safely airborne. The fashion show she was watching seemed to be super-slow, and she was dying to get to a phone and start dialling Scotland. Chewing her pencil impatiently, she looked down at her programme to see how far the 'Style Extravaganza', as the thing was billed, had progressed. With a sigh, she found they were less than halfway through.

Suddenly the lights dimmed until it was too dark to read, and the catwalk emptied. After a few seconds of breath-taking expectancy, the crackling over the speakers stopped and an orchestra burst forth with what Seraphina now knew only too well were the first few bars of 'O Sole Mio' by Luciano Pavarotti. Sinking down in her seat, she let out a little snort of frustration and was rewarded with a hard dig in the ribs from her mother.

Then a single spotlight went on and there was a loud gasp from the audience. Standing high on a podium, some three feet up from the stage, was a model wearing the most incredible outfit Seraphina had ever seen. Moving quickly, she picked up her pencil to write down a full description of the garment, but then stopped in mid-scribble as the truth dawned.

The outfit was really nothing special after all – just a few nondescript strips of some tweed stuff. What was out of this world, though, was the model wearing it. As he stepped down off his podium it was like seeing a

Greek god popping down to Earth on an awayday from Mount Olympus. Pens clattered to the floor all over the auditorium and jaws dropped like lead as one jaded, hackneyed writer after another realized they were in the presence of something rather perfectly-formed and special. As the spotlight gleamed across his short silvery-blond hair and over his tanned, athletic-looking body, a writer from the 'Daily Fashion Express' summed up what the majority of the audience were thinking. 'Good grief!' she shouted, huskily. 'They sure broke the mould when they made that one!'

When the show was over and the inevitable Spaghetti Bolognese was being served throughout the entire room, Seraphina watched with surprise as the model peered around the curtain by the side of the stage, spotted her sitting there, quietly sipping her Perrier, and darted across to take a seat at their table. With impeccable manners he shook hands and introduced himself before sitting down.

'Dolf Stollen,' he announced, bowing slightly as he took each hand. Then, swinging his designer rucksack off his shoulder, he eased himself into the empty chair next to Seraphina. With a little rush of pleasure she realized the model was staring at her, and as she turned to look back, she found her eyes locked in his. After a pause, during which Seraphina felt as though she'd been shot through with six thousand volts of electricity, Dolf smiled at her and tilted his head.

'You are English – no?' he asked.

'No – I mean yes!' Seraphina replied, totally confused and lost in his sapphire blue eyes.

'You should be German, like me,' Dolf went on, laughing. 'We have the same colouring exactly, do we not?'

Seraphina smiled – he was right.

'You are very beautiful, though. I saw you from the stage.' Seraphina blushed and Dolf went on, 'I had to find out who you were . . . you see, I . . .'

At that point Geraldine Foster-Brown, who had been twitching impatiently since Dolf arrived at the table, decided she had heard enough of his European chat-up. 'Why did you only grace the show with one appearance?' she asked, coldly. 'Is that all you get booked for?'

Dolf looked at her and a flicker of pride crossed his face. 'No!' he said, stiffly. 'I haff vat I zink you call zee principles. Ze rest of ze show iz not for me!'

Geraldine looked at him with surprise. 'Principles?' she asked. 'What about? Working too hard for a living? Do you have it written into your contracts that you must not be allowed to overtire yourself?'

'Nuzzin' like that,' Dolf told her, smiling with good-humour. 'I am a conzervationist. Look, zey know I vill not model zat stuff so zey put me in zis scene alone!'

Seraphina knew at once what Dolf was talking about. Most of the clothes in the show had been either made from or trimmed with fur or leather or snakeskin, and Dolf obviously shared her distaste at this sort of murder in the name of fashion. Smiling, she looked at him with a new respect in her eyes. 'Bravo, Dolf,' she said, toasting him with her mineral water, 'I agree with you one hundred per cent.'

Geraldine appeared to be seething. 'And I suppose you're going to tell me you're another teetotal, veg-etarian healthfood fiend, like my daughter, too!' she barked, taking a large bite out of the Parma ham on the plate in front of her.

Dolf turned to Seraphina in amazement. 'I can see

zat we haff more zan just our hair colour in common, if vat your mozzer says izz true!' he said, taking her hand and kissing it. 'So you haff zee principles, too – eh?'

Seraphina nodded happily. Dolf was turning out to be just too good to be true! For the rest of lunch they chewed lettuce leaves together and discussed their thoughts and tastes in everything from music to the theatre, and to their mutual amazement, found they coincided totally. Geraldine fumed and tutted as this musclebound German made obvious inroads to her daughter's affections, and after hearing Dolf make a date to take Seraphina to the opera the following evening, she exploded with impatience. Pulling her daughter up by the arm, she nodded curtly to Dolf and dragged Seraphina out by the scruff of the neck.

'I don't understand the problem!' Seraphina shouted as they collected their coats in the foyer. 'First you tell me you can't stand Terence because he's so rude and boorish, then you don't like Dolf, who is absolutely charming!'

'Yes – and a bit too charming for my liking!' Geraldine hissed back. 'Honestly, Seraphina, you'll have to start being a bit more careful with your choice of boyfriends – you'll be telling me next you really intend to go to the opera with that muscular creep in there!'

Seraphina's eyes blazed. She had been intending to back out of the date once all the fuss had died down, and she was already starting to feel guilty about letting Dolf chat her up while Terence was jetting his way to a lonely moor in the Scottish highlands, but her mother made her so angry that she decided to retaliate.

'Yes, of course I'm going!' she yelled. 'Dolf is

handsome and charming and very intelligent. I'm sure I'll have a wonderful time!'

And I'm sure you'll have a wonderful time, too! Geraldine thought, staring at her daughter as though she'd gone completely mad. 'Oh damn!' she muttered angrily. 'In all the rush to get out, I've left my notebook behind – I'll have to go back for it!'

'Do you want me to go for you?' Seraphina asked.

'No, no,' Geraldine murmured, tutting in annoyance, 'I'll go – you go out and call us a taxi. I won't be a minute.'

When Geraldine returned to their table Dolf was still sitting there, feet up and drinking a glass of red wine. 'Vell?' he asked, stuffing a forkful of ham into his mouth and chewing furiously. 'It vent OK, I zink – no?'

Geraldine looked down at him with a small smile of triumph. 'Yes,' she agreed, 'it all went very well. A couple of dates with you and my daughter will have forgotten all about Mr Thomas and his tripod! But don't forget,' she said, waggling her finger in front of Dolf's wonderfully straight, Greek-god nose, 'a couple of dates and that's all. If I find out you've so much as laid one beefy little finger on her you can forget that fashion spread with *Visage* I promised you and go back to that tin-pot model agency you belong to in Munich!'

Dolf stood up and bowed deeply. 'But of course,' he said, trying to kiss Geraldine's hand, but missing as she swirled off back to the foyer. 'Anyzing you say . . . absolutely anyzing!'

7

In-Flight Entertainment

Jeremy snored so loudly that he woke himself up. For a few seconds he had lost his bearings and wondered what the humming noise was, then he remembered he was still on the plane, and settled happily back in his seat again, tucking the warm woolly blanket the girls must've provided back under his chin again, and retracing his steps back to the Land of Nod.

As he started to doze, though, a nagging thought hit him – where were the girls? He'd never known them to be this quiet for so long. Opening one eye, Jeremy set about a quick fact-finding mission. The seats around him were empty. Curious, he looked round at Terence, but found the photographer was spark out under his own blanket. Then Jeremy heard a little noise from way down the plane behind him. It was a little hissing sound: 'Pssst, psst,' and it seemed to be getting louder with each 'Psst.' Thinking he'd heard some fatal leak in air pressure in the cabin, Jeremy wheeled round in alarm to inform the stewardess. What he saw when he turned, though, alarmed him a whole lot more. Bébé, Cherie, and Desirée were all up by the toilets, peeping round at him, blowing kisses and beckoning him to join them.

Jeremy looked around for moral support but a loud snore from Terence let him know he was on his own on this one. Swallowing hard he grinned stupidly and left his seat to wobble his way up the aisle, the girls hissing and cooing at him as he went. Finally he reached them.

'Well, then,' he said, with more bravado than he felt, 'what's all this about then?' Someone had once told him about something called 'the mile high club', and he hiccupped nervously, eyeing the toilets with alarm. He was so drunk he was still seeing a couple more Cheries than there were – or was it three Desirées? He wasn't altogether sure. At least they were still smiling at him, so he was safe for the time being.

Maybe it was the movement of the plane, or maybe it was an optical illusion, but Jeremy was sure the models were getting closer to him – too close, in fact. In a minute he wouldn't even have enough room to breathe! Giggling like a kid, Jeremy tried to sidestep them, but he got off-balance and they pushed him backwards, giggling more than he was. For a moment he thought he was falling into space, but then his bottom hit some sort of seat and he stopped praying for a parachute. To his horror he found he had fallen into the toilet, and to his further horror he watched as the girls followed him inside, locking the door behind them. The last sight he saw before blacking out was Cherie approaching him with a large pair of scissors in one hand and an evil gleam in her eyes, and he remembered hoping there was still a place for him in his old school's boy choir . . .

Seraphina gazed at Dolf across the candlelit dinner table and wondered for the umpteenth time how she got so lucky. All the other women diners in the restaurant had given her envious looks as she'd walked in clutching his arm, and even the fact that they'd eaten spaghetti while Luciano Pavarotti trilled in the background had done little to spoil the mood of the evening.

Dolf had turned up to collect her wearing a full dinner suit, including patent shoes, wing collar and spats, and clutching an enormous boxed orchid for her to pin on the front of her dress. In Italy, he told her, the men take their women, their food, and their opera very seriously so when in Rome . . . ?

Seraphina was delighted. Terence always wore jeans when he took her out and she was pleased to dress up herself for a change. Dashing back up to her room, she'd ripped off the silk shirt and baggy trousers she was wearing and reappeared downstairs some ten minutes later looking like a princess out of a fairy tale. Geraldine had insisted she packed a ballgown in case of emergencies, and now she was glad she had. The ice-blue silk it was made of matched Seraphina's eyes perfectly, and its tightly-laced, strapless bodice and full ripple-pleated skirt accentuated her narrow waist. As she strode down the large Victorian stairway of the hotel, pinning the orchid to her bodice, Dolf realized with a pang of regret that she would've put any of the models on the catwalks that week to shame.

'You look vonderful!' he told her, kissing her lightly on the side of the cheek. 'Absolutely beautiful! You vill zink it rude of me, but I vill haff to be staring at you all ze evening. You are ze most beautiful woman in Italy and I am ze luckiest man!'

Geraldine watched until they disappeared into the street, laughing and chattering about the opera they were going to see, then she pushed her bedroom door closed, smiling with satisfaction.

The evening was warm and balmy, and Dolf walked

71

Seraphina through a maze of enchanting little side streets, each one alive with its own shops or cafés or bars, until they came to the restaurant he had chosen for their meal. The place looked quite small from the outside, but as Seraphina stepped inside two narrow iron gates she found herself in a large, quiet courtyard that could've been miles out in the middle of the countryside, rather than in a street in the heart of Rome.

Steering her by the elbow, Dolf led Seraphina around a large, ancient-looking fountain and down a small flight of stone steps to a lower level. Here she found herself in what looked like a tiny orchard, except each tree was strung with silver fairy-lights, and under each tree stood a round table, laid for dinner, with two chairs. The place was more than two-thirds full, and a beaming waiter led them across the flagstones to a sheltered spot in the left-hand corner. The waiter pulled out a chair for Seraphina to sit down, tucked the napkin on her lap and shoved the menu in her hand before rushing off to organize the aperitif that Dolf had ordered.

'I know you don't drink,' he told Seraphina, smiling, 'but ze cocktails I haff ordered contain only ze slightest visper of alcohol – zey merely sluice ze glass out wiz it! I have ordered ze wholefood menu in advance, too, so zere is no need to read ze menu eizer!'

Seraphina relaxed – everything seemed to be taken care of, and she could just sit back and enjoy herself. She still felt a few little pangs of guilt when she thought of Terence, but it was a nice change to let someone else worry about the menu and organize the culture for the evening – with Terence, it was always she who had to do the planning and the bullying, otherwise they'd both spend every evening drinking pints down the pub!

The cocktails Dolf had chosen were delicious, and Seraphina was so thirsty after her busy day round the catwalks that she drank three in quick succession, then found herself singing along to the music of the quartet of strolling players that came round to their table to play love songs. Suddenly realizing she might be embarrassing Dolf, she glanced quickly across at him, but he seemed to be quite happy, smiling encouragement and filling her glass with what looked like very fizzy mineral water.

'This stuff tastes a bit off,' she said, taking a sip and wondering why Dolf's face was no longer in focus. 'Do you think I should send it back? Do you think I need glasses? My eyes keep going blurred!'

Dolf tasted her drink and smiled. 'I zink it is OK,' he told her. 'Ze more you drink, ze better it gets!' strangely enough, Seraphina found out he was right – it did taste better after the first glassful!

By the time they arrived at the opera Dolf had filled Seraphina with so much champagne that he had to sit with his hand over her mouth to stop her from joining in the singing there, too. 'Oh, Dolfy,' she slurred during the interval as they jostled with the rest of the audience in the queue for the bar, 'this is absolutely the very best piece of opera that I have ever heard in my entire life! Those fat guys on stage really know how to hold a note! And those costumes! Old Mo Polo would give his eye teeth to design something half as good . . .'

Floating home with the music of *'Aida'* ringing in her ears, Seraphina allowed herself to be taken as far as the lift before realizing she was in the wrong hotel.

'Dolf, Dolf!' she shouted. 'This is the wrong one – I'm not staying here!' But as she turned back towards him she saw he was getting a room key out of his pocket.

'Don't vorry,' he told her, patting her arm and drawing her closer to him. 'Zis iz my hotel – I zink you need a cup of coffee before your mozzer sees you – you look a little tired.'

Seraphina started to protest, but then realized Dolf was right – she did feel very tired. In fact it was all she could do to keep her eyes open. Smiling gratefully, she snuggled into his sleeve, amazed that anyone could be quite so clever and so handsome all at the same time.

The furniture in Dolf's room consisted of a small table and two single beds, so Seraphina sat gingerly on the edge of one of the beds while Dolf rang room service to order the coffee. Suddenly he was sitting down on the bed beside her, pushing her backwards on to the pillow and lifting her feet up so that she was lying down properly. Seraphina was pleased – her head felt too heavy and her feet were aching from all the walking she'd done that day, and Dolf obviously realized she'd be more comfortable like this. Why, he was even bending over to kiss her goodnight . . .

Suddenly, in her fuddled state, Seraphina remembered her phone call to Scotland and sat up with a start, just as Dolf was working out how to unlace her bodice. Grabbing the phone, she started to dial the number Terence had given her, but gave up when she discovered it had gone right out of her head.

'What are you doing, little one?' Dolf asked, giving up on the laces and planning a surprise attack from the kneecap upwards.

'Scotland . . . Scotland . . . I've got to make a phone

call . . .' Seraphina tried to say, but her voice was drowned out as Dolf covered her mouth with a string of nibbles and kisses.

'Vy you vant to ring Scotland?' he asked, seductively. 'Oo do you know zere oo vill be up at zis time off ze night?'

Seraphina looked at her watch. Dolf was quite right, Terry would be in bed now – it was three o'clock in the morning! Dolf was so clever, always right, even about the time . . .

As Dolf moved in for the kill, Seraphina was brought right to her senses – properly this time, although for a moment she couldn't work out why. Dolf had been leaning over her to turn out the bedside light and Seraphina's face had somehow come into contact with his breast pocket. It was then that she'd suddenly sobered up.

With a start, Seraphina realized what had done the trick. She had been met with a full blast of her mother's favourite perfume, so strong that for a minute she thought Geraldine had walked into the room! Peering into Dolf's pocket, she saw it was empty apart from the tickets to the opera and the envelope they had been in. Funnily enough, the envelope looked very similar to the sort her mother used, too! Sensing something was wrong, but too drunk to work out exactly what it might be, Seraphina slid out of Dolf's clutches and quickly phoned for a cab to take her back to her own hotel.

When Seraphina emerged for breakfast the next morning, tired, dazed, and obviously hung-over, Geraldine Foster-Brown made a mental note to have a very irate word with young Dolf – getting her daughter drunk had definitely not been part of the bargain!

'Enjoy yourself?' she asked her daughter, slicing the top off a lightly-boiled egg and heaping black pepper over the runny yolk.

Seraphina nodded dumbly. To be honest, she could hardly remember a thing that happened. All she knew for sure was that she had been taken out for a wonderful evening and had then proceeded to make a complete idiot of herself, singing in the restaurant and staggering about in the opera house. Dolf would probably never want to see her again – all the clinches in his hotel room and the discovery of her mother's envelope in his pocket had completely gone out of her head – she couldn't even remember how she'd managed to find her way home.

Geraldine sniffed loudly – her best line was yet to come. 'By the way,' she said, trying to sound offhand, 'Terence phoned here last night – several times, in fact! I told him you were out but that didn't stop him ringing as late as two o'clock in the morning and dragging me out of my bed!'

Seraphina looked up, miserable. 'Two o'clock?' she asked. 'What did he say when he found out I wasn't in at that time?'

'Oh, I don't know,' Geraldine replied, wiping her knife with the napkin before using it to spread honey over the slice of toast she was brandishing, 'I was too tired to remember – but I'll tell you one thing, he didn't sound at all pleased!'

As the plane taxied in at Aberdeen airport all the passengers got ready to disembark, but still there was no sign of Jeremy. Terence looked round worriedly – surely he hadn't fallen out halfway! The three models had poker faces and denied all knowledge of him, so in the end Terence had to tell the air stewardess.

'Look, luv, I know this sounds stupid, but I think we might be a man overboard! My party had another person with it when we took off, but since then he seems to have gone A.W.O.L.!' The stewardess looked at Terence suspiciously, but they were all ushered through to the terminal to wait while a thorough inspection of the plane was made.

After three-quarters of an hour Terence looked out of the viewing window to see a police car pull up by the plane and four policemen get out and stroll across the tarmac. The stewardess met them, waving her arms and pointing inside the cabin. 'Oh hell!' Terence said, running a hand through his hair and making for the boarding gate. 'I think he *has* fallen out – they've just sent for the police!' The three girls ran over to the window, giggling, as Terence raced out to see what had happened.

'Your friend is in the toilet,' the stewardess told him as he raced over to the plane.

'In the bog?' Terence repeated. 'What, has he got a jippy tummy, or did he get himself locked in?'

'Neither, I'm afraid,' one of the policemen said, coming over. 'It's more a case of "won't come out" than "can't come out" – does he have a history of mental illness, sir?'

Terence looked at the plane in bewilderment. 'Not as far as I know,' he said, trying to think hard, 'although he did tell me he used to like The Nolans at one time!'

'Would you like to have a word with him, sir?' the policeman continued. 'If he's a friend, you might be able to talk him out before we have to call the boys in.'

'The boys?' asked Terence.

'Well, yes. You see, this could be taken to be a sort of hijacking, sir,' the policeman said, squinting his eyes and rocking on his heels in a most impressive manner. 'He could be an international terrorist for all we know, all wired up with dynamite like a human time bomb!'

Terence gawped at the man. 'A human time bomb?' he asked, slack-jawed with disbelief. 'Our Jerry? No chance!'

'Jerry, sir?' the policeman asked, looking concerned. 'German gentleman, is he? Ever heard of the Bader Meinhoff, sir?'

Terence raced to the plane. 'I'll get him out!' he shouted. 'Tell your boys at the S.A.S. they can keep their hair on – they won't be needed this time!'

The toilet door looked flimsy enough but it didn't budge an inch when Terence rattled it hard. 'Oi, Jerry!' he called, trying to peep through the crack near the hinges. 'Git yourself out of that bog, mate! What's up? They're talking about lobbing in grenades in a minute – have you flipped your lid, or something?'

There was silence, then a rustling sound, then Jeremy's voice floated out. 'Terry! Is that you?'

'Well, who'd you think – Rambo or something?' Terence shouted back. 'What're you playing at?'

'Terry,' Jeremy warbled weakly, 'are you wearing trousers?'

Terence punched the door in exasperation. 'Well of course I am. Frightened I'm going to flash at you when you come out, are you? What's this – a new phobia about men in skirts?'

'No!' Jeremy called. 'It's just . . . well . . . can I have them, Terry? Could you take them off and slide them under the door, d'you think?'

Terence stared hard at the door as though hoping to acquire x-ray vision. 'My trousers?' he asked. 'What on earth . . . Oh, don't tell me you were so frightened of flying that you had a nasty accident with your . . .'

'It's those girls!' Jeremy hissed, angrily. 'They've got mine and gone! They pushed me in here and stripped my trousers off, and my pants, and they've stuck this bow thing on me with what seems like superglue . . . and . . . and . . .'

Terence understood at last. Roaring with laughter but stuffing his fists into his mouth so that Jeremy couldn't hear him, he clicked about with the walkie-talkie the policeman had given him, until a voice came over the other end. 'Yes sir?' it asked, sounding as though it had a peg on its nose. 'Do you need reinforcements?'

'Yes!' Terence told him. 'A large pair of underpants, please, and as soon as possible!'

And Terence sank to the floor, rocking with silent laughter – Jeremy wouldn't forget this trip in a hurry!

8

The Nightlite Club

Caroline offered to meet Melvin in a nearby wine bar for their evening out at the 'Nightlite' club, but Melvin was having none of that. 'I collect my women from their homes,' he told her, pulling himself up to his full height of five-feet-four-and-a-half-inches, 'and I insist on depositing them there at the end of the evening. It's what you might call a door-to-door service!'

Caroline smiled. 'OK, Melvin, you sweet old-fashioned chauvinist, what time do you intend calling on me?'

'Eight o'clock on the button!' Melvin announced, and he turned out to be as true as his word. As the clock hit eight Melvin's finger hit the buzzer – so precisely on the second, in fact, that Caroline knew he must've been waiting on the doorstep with a stopwatch.

As he made his way to her flat, she took one last look in the mirror to check her appearance. Debbie, one of her flatmates, had helped her choose the outfit, and she had to admit she was looking pretty good. Her hair had been dyed back to its normal colour again and she'd scrunch-dried it into a wild tangle of russet-coloured curls. Her dress consisted of a skin-tight black velvet sheath that fanned out into a black polka-dot netting fishtail from the knees downward. Vanessa Gimlette had generously lent her some diamanté jewellery and a pair of long black satin evening gloves, and for once she'd managed to apply her own make-up successfully. *Simon would go wild if he could see me now!* she thought to herself, then angrily pushed the idea to the back of her mind. Melvin was her partner tonight, not Simon, and a much nicer, more thoughtful person he was too. *Looks aren't everything*, she told herself firmly. *And anyway, Melvin isn't that bad – just because he's shorter than me and has a big bum and stocky legs, and his chest is a bit on the concave side* . . . The doorbell interrupted her thoughts, and she wiggled over in the tight dress to let Melvin in.

'Hi!' he announced, smiling happily. 'Whaddya think?'

Caroline took one look and nearly slammed the door again. What did she think? The dictionary hadn't been written that could come up with the suitable adjectives. Melvin's outfit left Caroline speechless. Over a shirt and tie of the most mind-bogglingly boring normality, Melvin was wearing what looked like a baseball jacket made out of tin-foil and shoe studs. A sort of silvery fringe dangled from one cuff of the monstrosity to the other, cowboy-style, and nestling in the well-gelled curls on the top of Melvin's head lurked a pair of Porsche sunglasses. With a kind of morbid fascination, Caroline took in the rest of the view. Below the waist Melvin was wearing his usual pair of baggy brown cords, but someone (his mother, probably) had piped the seams with matching silver piping, and the bottoms of the legs were tucked snugly away in a pair of black leather cuban-heeled cowboy boots.

Caroline felt physically sick. Her pride threshold was low, but Melvin had just managed to step over it. Pulling him into the flat before anyone else caught a glimpse, Caroline took a deep breath and had another look, hoping the ensemble wasn't as bad as it had looked at first glance. A second look told her it was –

if anything it was worse! Gary Glitter might've got away with it on a good day with the light behind him, but Melvin looked as though he'd strolled right out of the set of *Thunderbirds*.

'Melvin,' she squealed, 'the invite didn't say fancy dress! What on earth are you supposed to be?'

To Caroline's shame and horror, Melvin's face crumpled, and for a minute she thought he was going to cry. 'Fancy dress?' he asked. 'Who said anything about fancy dress?'

Caroline wished the ground would swallow her up as she realized he hadn't worn the outfit as a joke. 'Oh!' she blustered. 'I . . . er . . . um . . . I didn't mean . . . that is, I was only joking, Melvin . . . er . . . you look . . . um . . . fine! Really trendy!'

Melvin's eyes shone. 'Really?' he asked. 'You're not just saying that? I did wonder whether it was just a bit too fashionable for tonight, but then I remembered you saying there were going to be pop stars there and everything, so I decided to go for broke! You look great, too,' he finished, managing to drag his eyes away from his own reflection at last.

At that moment the door to the kitchen opened and Debbie walked out. She looked at Melvin for a long time, face totally emotionless, then she looked over at Caroline. Finally she looked back at Melvin and then, without a word, backed slowly into the kitchen again. As the door closed behind her Caroline could hear muffled choking sounds and she turned on the radio to drown out the hysterical laughter that she knew would follow. 'Right, Melvin!' she said, brightly, 'we'll be off then!' and taking one tin-foiled arm in her own she set off towards the lift.

The 'Nightlite' club turned out to be everything

Caroline had hoped – and more. There was a small bit of bother on the way in, when a burly, brylcreemed bouncer had let her through, then planted a beefy fist on Melvin's chest to bar his access, but once she'd fished both of the invites out of her bag Melvin had sailed through without too much bother.

Once inside they paused to admire the foyer, which was decorated to look like a spider's nest, complete with hanging webs and huge dangling black widow spiders, before following the source of the music they could hear blasting out of the main dance-floor area. A crowd of people were queueing for tables, and Caroline felt a small buzz of excitement as she recognized writers from all the top magazines and newspapers. Thrilled, she turned around to point some out to Melvin, but he was looking around anxiously. At last he seemed to have spotted what he was looking for. 'Just off to point Percy at the porcelain!' he yelled at the top of his lungs, just as the record finished and there was a break in the music. As Melvin shot off, red-faced, he left Caroline standing by herself, deep in a pool of utter embarrassment, as the other people giggled and sniggered at her.

By the time Melvin got back, Caroline had found their table and was peering round to see if she could recognize any celebrities in the place.

'Guess who was in the loo!' he shouted, easing himself into the chair beside her and nearly pulling the tablecloth off the table in the process.

'Do tell!' Caroline said, clutching her glass and lifting it out of harm's way at the last minute.

'Logan Wong, the top fashion photographer!' Melvin told her. 'He's about the greatest photographer alive and he actually let me share the roller-towel with him!'

'Look!' Caroline yelled, tugging at Melvin's silver fringing. 'Down there, by the dance-floor! Isn't that Rory LeMal? He looks beautiful! And he's with his girlfriend, that model – Laura somebody-or-other!'

'Laura Evans,' Melvin told her. 'She was down in the studio last week – I think Terence was shooting her for a cover. She's absolutely gorgeous!'

Caroline and Melvin watched the rock star and his girlfriend as they danced together, laughing happily and obviously very much in love. Caroline sighed – if only she and Simon could be like that! Taking a large swig of her free press-only pink champagne, Caroline stood up quickly and turned to Melvin. 'Come on,' she said, bravely, 'we're going to dance! It's not only super-glam rock stars and their ultra-smoothie model girlfriends that can chuck it about a bit!'

Five minutes later Caroline was deeply regretting acting on impulse. Melvin danced about as well as he dressed and the other dancers had cleared a little space on the floor to appreciate his antics from a safe distance. Eyes closed and tongue out, Melvin writhed and gyrated, jiggling his silver fringe and kicking up his cowboy boots like Roy Rogers with the St Vitus dance. Caroline bounced about politely, hoping that no one would take them for a pair, but every time she tried to sneak back to her seat Melvin would grab her round the waist before she could escape, spinning her round with a wild whoop of pleasure as though they'd been rehearsing the routine for months. At last a U2 record came on and even Melvin had to know when he was licked. Slipping his arm around Caroline's waist he ushered her back to their seats, wiping perspiration off his forehead as he did so.

To their surprise they found Vanessa Gimlette sitting

waiting for them. 'Hi, kiddos!' she shouted, waving a
black denim and red sequin-clad hand in their direction. 'Sit down and tell all! Who's here of any note?
Anyone to get excited about or just the usual hangers-
on of the cast of Eastenders?' When she caught sight
of Melvin, Caroline thought she was going to swallow
her teeth!

'Melv!' she spluttered. 'So you were that human
dynamo I caught sight of writhing away under the
spotlights just now! What's the look supposed to be, in
case my readers enquire? Rhinestone Cowboy or The
Urban Spaceman?'

As soon as Melvin's back was turned Vanessa dug
Caroline in the ribs. 'You came with that?' she
mouthed, eyes wide with disbelief. Vanessa, it turned
out, had come with not one but three escorts, all
wonderfully-dressed and devastatingly-handsome, and
all three quite happy to chat amongst themselves while
Caroline and Vanessa discussed work.

'Has Dottie told you who's getting the proper job at
the mag yet?' Vanessa asked, stirring the bubbles out
of her champagne and taking a tentative sip.

'No,' Caroline told her, 'we haven't heard a peep
from her yet – it's all getting a bit nervewracking! I
thought I was well out of the running till that interview
with the princess came along, but I still think Seraphina
stands the better chance.'

Vanessa opened her mouth to say something, then
appeared to think better of it. 'I didn't get a chance to
congratulate you about that interview,' she said at last.
'It was incredible luck – Geraldine was seething for
days!' Caroline smiled modestly.

'Little Melvin's pics weren't bad either, come to
that,' Vanessa went on. 'Found out which way up to

hold the camera at last, has he?' Caroline smothered a giggle and looked anxiously at Melvin, but he was quite happy explaining the finer points of colour processing to Vanessa's toy-boys and appeared to be well out of earshot.

'Look,' Vanessa went on, 'I know I shouldn't be saying this, and you must promise not to breathe a word to anyone, but I really wouldn't break my neck trying for a steady job with *Visage* if I were you.'

Caroline turned to look at her. 'Why ever not?' she asked, suddenly curious.

'Well, it's only a small rumour at the moment,' Vanessa said, keeping her voice low, 'but you know what they say about no smoke without fire – I happened to be passing Dottie's office the other day and I overheard . . .' but at that moment an enormous burst of loud disco music sent Melvin spinning to his feet, and he grabbed Caroline's arm, yanking her off her chair and on to the dance-floor.

'Melvin!' she yelled, angry at being interrupted so rudely. 'I was just . . .' but Melvin was gone. The pounding rhythms had reached his spinal column and he was leaping and twitching for all he was worth. With a large sigh of submission, Caroline closed her eyes, stuck out her tongue, and joined in for all she was worth.

As a slow, romantic number began and Melvin lunged sweatily towards her, Caroline felt her arm grabbed by a cooler, firmer hand. Turning quickly to find out who the icy grip belonged to, Caroline found herself staring at Simon's handsome, determined-looking features.

'Simon!' she gasped, as Melvin grabbed her other

arm, and for a moment she thought the two men were going to play tug-o'-war with her.

'Caroline!' Simon said, ignoring Melvin and pulling her closer to him. 'I thought you might be here tonight. Look, I must talk to you!'

Caroline tossed her head. 'I don't think we have much to say to one another,' she told him haughtily. 'Surely you've humiliated me enough for the time being!' Melvin started to pull her in the other direction. 'Let go of my arm!' Caroline screamed, and Melvin dropped it like a hot brick, blinking hard with fear. 'Both of you!' Caroline added, turning to Simon with a cold stare. He did as he was told, too.

Suddenly Simon looked across at Melvin and smirked slightly. 'You haven't introduced me,' he said, leaning across and extending his hand. 'This must be the new boyfriend, Caroline! Pleased to meet you – I'm Simon Moorhouse, Caroline's flatmate.'

'Simon lives in the flat upstairs,' Caroline cut in angrily, 'when he's not out on the town with every sexy-looking blonde from here to Shepherd's Bush, that is!'

Melvin looked puzzled – there was something going on here that he seemed to be missing. Why did Caroline shake her head so hard when this Simon asked if he were her boyfriend? And if this was the same Simon that Caroline'd been ranting on about for weeks, why was she being so hostile towards him? Melvin decided this had to be a different bloke with the same name.

As Melvin stood pondering, Simon grabbed Caroline and pushed her firmly off the dance-floor and well away from the main crowd. 'Look, Caroline,' he said as she wheeled on him angrily, 'I'm sorry to be so rough, but I needed to explain something. I've only just read that letter you sent me – don't you remember seeing how I let my mail pile up? I just wanted to let you know how sorry I am to have distrusted you, that's all. I thought you were being stupid and two-faced, but now I realize I was wrong. Please forgive me!'

Caroline looked up at Simon and he pulled her so close that she could feel his heart beating through his shirt. 'You look so beautiful,' he said, simply. 'Please don't be angry with me – I hoped we could be friends.'

Totally confused and mesmerized by the sight of the face she had wanted for so long hovering close to her own, Caroline closed her eyes and felt Simon kiss her gently on the lips. Head spinning, she felt herself clinging to him as the kiss got harder and his body leant against hers, crushing her against the wall.

Suddenly Caroline came to her senses and, mustering all her strength, she pushed Simon away. 'No!' she shouted as he stepped backwards. 'I don't want to become one of your army of Barbie-dolls! I don't want to see my letters getting lost among the mountain of mail from your other admirers – and I don't want my flowers snatched away by someone who thinks I work for Interflora, either! Leave me alone, Simon. You've got enough admirers already – why do you want one more to make a fool of?'

Simon turned pale. 'You don't understand, do you, Caroline? All I want is . . .' but Simon suddenly seemed to collapse at the kneecaps, falling forwards with a look of utter surprise on his face. As he sank to the floor Melvin was revealed, standing behind with a victorious smile on his face.

'Was that smarmy creep annoying you?' he asked an amazed Caroline. 'I saw him making a pest of himself, kissing you like that, and when I saw you fighting him off I decided I'd better come to your rescue!'

'What did you do to him?' Caroline asked, looking down at the floor.

'Oh – it's an old trick tiny guys like myself have to learn very early on,' Melvin said, airily. 'Come up behind them and chop them down at the kneecaps – go down like a deadwood tree every time!'

As Simon staggered to his feet a tall, willowy blonde rushed out of the ladies' loo with a little yelp and rushed over to grab his elbow. 'Simon, darling – are you alright? Is it your heart or something?' she twittered.

Caroline caught his eye as he pulled himself up. 'Not another one?' she whispered. Then, smiling brightly, she took Melvin's arm and let him lead her back to the dance-floor.

9
Happy Campers

Terence Thomas cleared his throat and tried to launch into what sounded like a logical explanation. 'Well, Dottie,' he began, twiddling the telephone wire nervously, 'we . . . er . . . that is . . . I . . . um . . .'

He covered the mouthpiece with one hand and gazed at the naked bulb in the ceiling of the phone booth for inspiration. A loud squeaking noise in his right ear brought him back to earth with a bump. Dottie was getting impatient.

'What's up?' she squealed. 'You should've been back by now! Where the hell are you?' Terence looked about him gloomily. *Good question!* he thought.

All around the phone box the Scottish mists were rising like dry ice, and through the grey murk he could just make out a strange, hunched, spectral form, rising up like Banquo's ghost and wailing like a banshee. 'Hold on Dot!' Terence yelled into the mouthpiece, and he kicked the door to the booth open with one foot. 'Any luck?' he asked the wraith, but it shook its head slowly and turned back to the moors.

'Sorry, Dottie,' Terence explained. 'That was Jeremy – I thought he might've found the girls.'

'Found them?' Dottie's voice shrieked back over miles of British Telecom cable. 'Where did you lose them?'

'Ah . . . good question,' Terence said sheepishly, sweating hard despite the frosty weather. 'We haven't actually lost the models, Dottie. That is, not really

90

. . . it's just that the shoot is going so well we . . . we wondered whether we could stay up here a few more days to . . .'

Terence looked at Jeremy's misery-ridden face, peering through a small patch he'd wiped clear in the glass. Suddenly all the mock-bravado sank out of his voice. In one of those earth-shattering, mind-boggling, life-altering decisions that you sometimes have to make at the drop of a hat, Terence decided to tell Dottie the truth about the whole fiasco.

The drive from the airport had been a nightmare. As the hired car sped down one winding heather-strewn country lane after another, the tension inside it had built up to the point where the hairs on the back of Terence's neck began to stand on end. Jeremy hadn't moved a muscle. Sitting bold upwards in the front passenger seat, he stared out of the window as though on the alert for Scottish highwaymen. The three models were crammed into the back of the car, and they were strangely silent too, apart from the occasional snapping of bubble gum and the odd snigger which would be instantly muffled.

Finally, Terence pulled the car up in what looked like an empty field and turned off the engine, plunging them all into even deeper silence. 'Well,' he said, eventually, 'we're here!'

Cherie wound her window down and peered out. 'I don't see any hotel,' she said. 'Are you sure we aren't lost? D'ya wanna check on your map again, Terry? This is a real dead-and-alive hole!'

'Nope,' Terence said, opening his door and climbing out, 'this is it alright! Clachan of Campsie, right in the heart of the Campsie Fells – slap bang in the middle of nowhere, like you were promised! What were you expecting – Seaview Guest House, or Dunromin' or something? When *Visage* promise you a remote location, they mean it! We don't pop you in a nice warm studio with a wind machine and cardboard cows for a backdrop, you know. This is the real McCoy!'

'But where do we sleep?' Desirée wailed, clutching her quilted baseball jacket around her shoulders and shivering. 'This place gives me the creeps, Terry!'

'Yeah,' Bébé joined in. 'Where d'we crash out? It's been a long journey an' I wanna shower an' eats! Let's check in at a hotel somewhere – I don' wanna stare at some stupid ol' field! We can go location-huntin' tomorrow!'

Terence turned to the girls with a sickly grin on his face. 'Like I said,' he told them, 'this is it – this is where we're staying. There's no hotel around for miles, so we're going to have to kip down on site! It's only for a couple of nights,' he added. 'You'll soon be back in civilization again.'

'You mean we have to sleep in the car?' Desirée squawked, eyes bulging with disbelief. 'There's not enough room to swing a cat on that back seat, let alone sleep three models!'

Terence looked about anxiously. 'Oh no,' he said, with more confidence than he felt right at that moment. 'Sleeping quarters've been arranged – some local farmer has agreed to put us all up. He should be here waiting for us now, but maybe we're a bit early. No problem,' he smiled, leaping into action. 'We can wait in the car, the heater's working so we'll keep quite warm.'

It was a full hour before the farmer's face appeared at Terence's side window, making him jump as it loomed up out of the mist that had formed. By that time the girls had started teasing Jeremy again, and the car was rocking with their shrieks of laughter.

'You therr crrowd frrom London?' a voice barked out of nowhere. Terence shot out of his seat, nearly concussing himself on the windscreen in the process.

'Yeah – that's us,' he said, clambering out of the car and looking at the man with relief. 'You must be Mr McClancy – the one with the farm, right?'

The old man nodded sharply, his mouth closed so firmly that his jaw looked as though it'd been wired shut. He looked at the models in the car suspiciously, then glared back at Terence.

'Er, where is the farm?' Terence asked after a long pause, during which the icy gusts of wind had made his lips turn blue. 'I think the girls would like to get their heads down – it's been quite a long day.'

The farmer stared at him hard. 'Farrm?' he asked. 'Yeirr no atta farrm, ye know. Ma farrm's a way too farr fer ye. Ye'rr stayin' at ma park, ye' know.'

Terence slammed the car door quickly, before the girls caught any of the conversation. 'At your park?' he asked, shivering. 'What do you mean, exactly? What sort of park?'

'Ma mobile homes – ma caravan park, o' course!' the man said, eyeing Terence as though he'd flipped his lid. 'Ye've two reserved, altho' ah must admit it's a wee bit off the season now, an' th' others arrr all empty, anyway. Didya no see them as ye drove in?' and he waved an arm proudly towards a section of field towards the left of the car.

Terence looked in that direction and found to his astonishment that the farmer was right – what he'd taken at a glance to be four rather large cows huddled together in the distance were in fact a herd of extremely small run-down-looking caravans grouped around a derelict corrugated iron hut. 'All th' comforts off home,' the farmer was announcing, 'we'rrr verrry popular with the tourists during the season, you know. Toilet facilities and showers arrr commmunal, of course, an' there's spare blankets in case ye feel th' chill!'

Terence looked at the four figures huddled in the car. It would take more than spare blankets to thaw that lot out! 'Thanks!' he said weakly. 'Thanks a lot. I'm . . . I'm er, sure we'll be very comfortable. Is there . . . er . . . anywhere we might get some food?'

'All taken care of!' the farmer snapped, turning back for his trek home across the fields. 'Ah've left yerrr supplies inside th' vans ferrr ye!' and with a quick swirl of the sporran and squelch of the gumboots he strode off into the mist and was gone.

Terence was relieved to find that the girls took the news of their mobile homes quite well. All three dived into the nearest caravan and inspected the inside with a chorus of little whoops and yells. 'Hey, it's so quaint!' Bébé shouted from one of the windows. 'It even has little plastic flowers in little plastic vases on the window ledges!'

'And the mattresses on the beds are all covered in this funny fabric!' Desirée yelled. 'It has this cute green pattern all over it!'

'I think that's what we in this country call mould,' Terence muttered under his breath, unpacking his camera gear and inspecting the caravan he'd be using with rising depression. Jeremy, he noticed, had pottered off into the one that stood furthest away from the models' sleeping quarters. Suddenly there was

94

silence from across the field and Terence looked out to see what was wrong.

'Tereeee!' Cherie shouted, looking panic-stricken. 'There are no toilets in this caravan! I hope you don't expect us to go behind a bush or something – there might be wild animals out there!'

Terence walked over to inspect the corrugated-iron hut and had his worst fears confirmed as he pulled the wooden door open. Standing inside were two cobweb-covered toilets, and hanging from one wall was what he supposed must be the shower units. 'You're OK!' he announced, cheerily. 'They're all in there! Not exactly the Ritz, but it should be quite good fun roughing it for a couple of days, eh?'

Jeremy sank down on to his bed cautiously. He was still red raw from the glue that had held the bow in place, but his pride was hurting most of all. He knew he'd deserved a revenge attack after trying to con the models into believing he was in charge of model bookings at *Visage*, but he also knew he'd have to get his own back in some small way if the entire job wasn't going to be spent with them giggling and snorting every time he got within eyesight.

As the wind howled and moaned around his caravan, Jeremy plotted his revenge. Nothing too nasty he thought, turning over several possibilities in his mind, just something quick and funny – something to make them look a bit stupid, but something harmless enough to let them see the joke too. Then Jeremy heard giggling outside his caravan, and he peered out of the window to watch all three girls, wrapped only in bathtowels, pick their way laughing and screaming across the thistly path to the grim little washroom. Jeremy looked at the models, then he looked at their

95

caravan, realizing with a grin that the perfect idea had just been handed to him on a plate. Maybe this trip would be fun, after all, he thought to himself.

Terence woke up the following morning at dawn, just as the first rays of a weak and watery sun filtered through the thick dust that covered the caravan window. 'Perfect!' he thought, jumping out of his damp-riddled bed and peering at the sky. 'Just perfect!'

Dottie had asked him to get some shots of the girls looking wild and modern against a faded, ancient Scottish background, and he knew that in about one hour the pale light would be hitting the dew and the mists with just enough strength to get the mysterious sort of atmosphere he wanted. Pulling on a pair of jeans he leapt out of the caravan and raced across to alert the others. There was a faint sign of life from Jeremy's caravan as he thumped on the door, but the girls all appeared to be sounder sleepers. As Jeremy's bleary-looking head appeared through his window, Terence called to him to wake the girls up while he sorted out the gear he'd be needing.

As he rushed to load the car up, though, Terence suddenly stopped in his tracks and froze, rooted to the spot. Where the car had been standing the night before there was now nothing but grass and air. Terence stared, totally confused. In London he would've immediately assumed the thing had been nicked, but here in the Scottish countryside with no one around for miles apart from a handful of dozy-looking cows? Puzzled, he went across to inspect the area more closely. There was an oblong-shaped dry patch on the grass to prove where the car had been, so where was it now?

Suddenly worried that he might've left the handbrake off, Terence raced over to the side of the hill, but to his relief there were no crumpled wrecks standing at the base of the slope. 'Jeremy!' he thought quickly, and raced back to the caravans to see whether he could throw some light on the problem.

To his surprise Jeremy was exactly where he had just left him, head hanging out of the window and a dazed expression on his face. 'Jeremy!' Terence shouted, exasperated. 'The car! It's gone!' Jeremy looked very white and very guilty. 'Have you moved it, mate?' Terence asked, panting. 'Hurry up, I'm going spare here!'

Jeremy looked at Terence and shrugged. 'No!' he said, eyes darting about shiftily. 'Haven't touched it! Maybe . . . maybe it's been nicked or something!'

'What, out here?' Terence asked doubtfully, 'There's no one around to nick it! Here – hang about, I wonder if one of the girls took it to go shopping or something! Did you get any answer from them?' Jeremy's head disappeared as Terence shot over to bang on the models' caravan door again. To his surprise there was total silence inside it. 'Hey! Come on, you lot!' he yelled, leaping up to look in the windows. 'What've you done with the car? Has one of you borrowed it? What're you up to this time?'

Jeremy appeared behind him, chewing his nails. 'I . . . er . . . don't think they're in there, Terry,' he said, slowly.

Terence wheeled round, eyes popping. 'Whaddya mean, they're not in there?' he asked. 'Where are they – in the loo?' and he strode across to bang on the door of the hut. Jeremy followed him.

'I . . . er . . . don't think they're in there either, Terry,' he said, quietly.

'Then where the hell are they?' Terence asked, exploding with impatience. 'I want them up and ready to pose for some shots in about fifteen minutes' time – the light'll be perfect then. What're they up to? I knew we should've booked girls we'd used before, this lot are going to be more trouble than they're worth!' Suddenly he remembered Jeremy's guilty-looking face. 'What've you been up to?' he asked, grabbing Jeremy by the scruff off the neck, 'You know where they've gone, don't you?'

Jeremy turned as white as a sheet. 'Yes – I mean no!' he spluttered. 'That is, well, I don't know *where* they've gone, but I might know *why*!'

Terence put him down again. 'OK!' he shouted. 'Let's hear it. What's monkey-brain been up to this time?'

Jeremy pulled a small rusty key out of his pocket. 'All I did,' he explained, 'was to lock their door. It was only for a laugh.'

Terence snatched the key angrily and raced up the steps to the models' caravan. Unlocking the door he peered inside. 'Come on, girls!' he called. 'You can come out now – I've unlocked the door!'

Jeremy caught up with him. 'They . . . er . . . they weren't inside the caravan when I locked the door,' he mumbled.

'You locked them out?' Terence yelled. 'In this weather?'

'Yes, but only for a laugh,' Jeremy told him. 'I was waiting for them to come hammering on my caravan door as soon as they'd realized what I'd done, then I would've given them the key – honest!'

'So what happened?' Terence asked.

'I . . . I . . . fell asleep,' Jeremy confessed. 'So I don't know what they did when they found they were locked out!'

'What they did,' Terence told him, 'was to take the car and clear off!' Then he stopped as a sudden thought hit him. 'Where exactly were the girls when you locked them out?' he asked. 'How did you catch all three outside at once?'

Jeremy looked scared. 'They were taking a shower,' he said.

'And what exactly were they wearing?' Terence cut in.

'Just their towels,' Jeremy said quietly, shuffling his feet as he waited for the explosion.

'Bathtowels!' Terence shouted. 'You locked them out while they were dripping wet and half naked! They could've died of exposure in this weather! No wonder they took the car – I just hope they hurry up bringing it back!' and he stomped off across the field to see if he could spot the car in the distance anywhere.

It was a full five hours before Terence and Jeremy realized the models weren't coming back, and neither was the car. Annoyance gave way to worry and worry turned into panic as it began to get dark and they found out they were stranded. As the winds whistled round the caravan Terence shivered inside his spare blanket and cursed Jeremy with every fibre of his being.

'How could you be so stupid!' he shouted. 'A joke's a joke and I'm the first one to join in, but we could die out here, without food or transport! That's if we don't freeze to death first,' he added. 'We're miles from anywhere and all we've got between us is a thermos of luke-warm porridge and a couple of rock-hard oat cakes that Rob Roy left us! I just hope my dentist's got my dental records up to date so's they can identify the skeletons when they finally find us. I'd hate to think they might get your bones confused with mine!'

Jeremy shuddered – starving to death sounded quite painless compared to the fate he would have to face if Dottie got her hands on him!

Suddenly a quiet chugging noise in the distance brought them both to their feet. 'Thank God!' Terence shouted. 'They've come back at last!' and he rushed to the door to catch the car coming up the path. When he peered out into the darkness though, he gradually realized that the sound that was growing nearer was a lot different to the steady purring of the engine of a car. At last, with a loud slurp of mud and a heavy chugging sound, a battered old tractor wobbled into view. As it pulled up in front of them, a pair of slime-covered gumboots dangled over the side and the farmer jumped down. He looked at Terence and Jeremy silently for a minute, then let out a short, cackly dry laugh. 'Off then, arrrre they?' he asked, cocking his head like a bird and smiling broadly.

Jeremy realized he meant the girls. 'Yes . . . we had a bit of a problem. They accidentally got locked out and . . .'

'Mad wi' ye, they were!' the farmer went on, ignoring him.

'You've seen them?' Terence asked. 'Where are they? Where's the car?'

'Oh – aboot twenty miles or sooo away be now, I should think!' the farmer told him, chuckling. 'If they took my advice an' booked in at th' nearest four-star

100

hotel, that is!' he added. 'Passed them on the road last night – an' a sorry sight they looked too, all drippin' wet, they were! Asked me to direct them to th' nearest hotel an' I was happy to oblige.'

Terry's head reeled. 'Four star hotel?' he asked.

'Aye, an' they gave me this note in case ah saw ye today,' the farmer said, handing Terence a scrap of paper.

'*Dear Boys,*' it read. '*Sorry to quit so suddenly, but we know you like your beauty sleep and we didn't want to disturb you late at night. Have booked into a smart little place to dry out (sure Visage will foot the bill!) and will wait for you here. Love, the girls.*'

Terence looked at the farmer. 'Could you take us to the hotel to pick them up?' he asked. 'We're stranded without transport.'

The farmer cackled again, clutching his sides. 'Twenty miles?' he asked. 'On this thing?' and he patted his tractor fondly. 'Ye're jokin' off courrse! Ah might just manage it as farrr as a telephone, but tha's the lot – ye're on yerrr own afffter thait!'

Terence paused at the end of his story and waited for Dottie's onslaught. Fortunately, after only twenty seconds of abuse and death threats, his money ran out and they were cut off. He reeled out of the booth, Dottie's voice still ringing in his ears.

'What'd she say?' Jeremy asked, looking worried. 'Did she mind? Was she angry?'

'Mind?' Terence told him. 'Angry? No – I don't think those words fit the bill adequately! Dottie was demented, Jeremy – out of her skull with wrath! Foaming at the mouth and oozing from the ears! She wants your head, mate – on a plate, with an apple in its mouth!' And Terence strode off to try to find civilization, Jeremy ambling miserably behind in his wake.

10
Many Happy Returns

'Seraphina?'

'Terry!' Seraphina could hardly believe how much she buckled at the knees at the sound of Terence's voice over the telephone. He sounded tired and worried, and with a sudden flood of feelings she realized she was falling in love with him. 'How are you?' she asked, stuck for words and knowing the entire office was eavesdropping.

'OK,' he told her, and this time he sounded rather cold and distant.

'Good.' Geraldine Foster-Brown looked up from the proofs she was reading and watched her daughter carefully. Seraphina had turned as red as a radish and had started to look unsure of herself. Geraldine smiled – her little plan seemed to be working already. Normally Seraphina and Terence nattered non-stop when they got together on the phone.

'I'm OK, too,' Seraphina said, after a long pause.

'Good,' Terence replied.

'Did you . . . ?' 'Are you . . . ?' they both began at once, then stopped again.

'Where are you?' Seraphina asked. 'You sound as if you're miles away.'

'I'm downstairs in the studio,' Terence told her.

'Downstairs?' Seraphina yelled. 'Now?'

'Yeah,' Terence replied, 'looks like it.'

Why didn't you come up to see me? Seraphina wanted to ask him, but she wouldn't give her mother the gratification of listening to them argue. Instead, her eyes filled with tears and she leant over her desk, hair covering her face, and pretended to be reading.

'Have a good time in Italy?' Terence asked eventually, and even over the phone Seraphina could hear the bitter edge to his voice.

'Yes, it was quite good fun,' Seraphina told him, trying to keep a light tone to her voice. 'We worked very hard, though – rushing about from one collection to another. I hardly had time to see anything of the country at all!'

'Burning the candle at both ends, then?' Terence asked, and Seraphina knew the question was loaded.

'Not really,' she said, carefully. 'We went out a couple of times for meals but I was usually too tired to paint the town red or anything.'

'We?' Terence asked her.

'Yes – my mother and I. We mostly stuck together out there, although we did meet up with a few people from the fashion business that we knew.'

'So how come these quiet little meals went on till three o'clock in the morning, Seraphina?' Terence asked, still keeping his voice even although his stomach was knotting up with jealousy and anger. 'And how come your mother answered the phone every time I called, if the two of you were sticking so closely together out there? She didn't even seem to know where you were, let alone who you were with, although she didn't mind dropping heavy hints that you weren't exactly out on a hen night! My God, Seraphina, I had to walk twenty-odd miles through a ploughed field every time, just to hear your mother gloating! What exactly were you up to out there?'

Seraphina glowered at her mother, who was innocently pretending to be sticking stamps on to envelopes and who smiled sweetly at her from across the office. Suddenly all the stories Geraldine had been telling her about Terence's trip to Scotland filtered back into her head. 'What was I up to?' she asked, still trying to whisper but hissing through her teeth. 'Me? What about you? Sharing a caravan with three American sex-pots! Cavorting about half-naked on the moors, and then chasing them off to some luxury hotel somewhere to finish the job! And you've got the nerve to ask me what I've been up to? Honestly, Terry!'

Geraldine leant slowly back in her chair, happy that her scheme seemed to be even more effective than she'd hoped. *Talk your way out of that one, medallion-man!* she thought, humming happily.

Terence, much to Seraphina's surprise and anger, was laughing fit to bust. Hurt and humiliated, she looked at Geraldine's smug smile and listened to Terence's manic laughter, then slammed the phone down hard. 'Problems, darling?' Geraldine asked, but the question fell on deaf ears. Seraphina barged out of the office, choking back a sob, and set off to speak to Terence in person.

Jeremy and Caroline looked across at one another with mild surprise. 'She must be in love,' Caroline said, watching the door swinging on its hinges after Seraphina's dramatic exit. 'I've never seen her behave like that before – she's usually so cool and calm about everything.'

'Stupid,' Jeremy agreed, letting out what he hoped sounded like a scoffing laugh. 'Rots yer brain cells, that sort of behaviour! Should've thought old Terry would've known better than to get himself involved in all that heavy sort of rubbish, too!'

'What "heavy sort of rubbish", Jeremy?' Caroline asked with a slightest tinge of irritation in her voice.

'Oh, you know, all that Mills and Boon bilge – turns you into a walking zombie! He'll be reciting poetry to her next and sending her bunches of flowers! Mind you,' he added, laughing, 'if she's caught wind of what went on in Scotland our Terry could be for the high jump!'

'And what exactly did go on up there, Jeremy?' Caroline asked, leaning across the desk and planting her elbow firmly in the centre of his packet of foil-wrapped banana sandwiches.

'Well . . . you know!' Jeremy said, trying to wink.

'No, Jeremy, I don't know,' Caroline said. 'Do tell.'

'Well . . . locked away up there in that tiny caravan with only three buxom beauties for company, Caroline, what d' you think? I mean, "a man's got to do what a man's got to do" and all that, eh?'

Caroline's face had turned into a mask. '*That* tiny caravan?' she asked.

'Well . . . not exactly one caravan. More like . . . two, but . . .'

'Or maybe even four or five of them?' Caroline cut in loudly. 'Although it didn't really matter how many caravans there were, seeing as how there was only you and Terence to sleep in them, eh, Jeremy? And seeing as how you had no models up there at all owing to your stupid little joke that backfired, eh, Jeremy? So what exactly did "a man have to do" up there all alone in the middle of a freezing cold empty field – count the cows all night? Or were there a few sheep up there to keep you company? Eh?'

Jeremy's face reddened. For some reason unknown to himself he'd wanted to impress Caroline and maybe even make her feel jealous, but it seemed Terry had already been shooting his mouth off about their disastrous trip. All Jeremy hoped was that he hadn't told her about the incident in the aeroplane loo, or he'd never be able to go to the toilet at work without thinking she was laughing at him.

'So how're things with darling Simon since I've been away?' he asked, shutting Caroline up in the quickest, most effective way he knew how. To his surprise though, her face didn't twitch a muscle.

'Simon?' she asked, looking as though the name rang a faint bell. 'He's fine – I suppose. Why d'you ask?'

Jeremy was shocked. Just the mention of that moron's name would've had Caroline blushing and chewing her lip a week ago – what'd been going on in the meantime? With a sudden pang he wondered whether Simple Simon'd finally got his act together and asked Caroline out on a date. Just the thought was enough to make Jeremy angry. 'Don't tell me you took him to that ball at the "Nightlite" – not that miserable drongo! What'd he do all evening – lecture you on your grammar and tell you to scrub off all your make-up? Did you manage to stay awake while he discussed James Joyce and D. H. Lawrence, or did he just take you along to keep his tribe of blonde groupies in check?'

To Jeremy's utter amazement Caroline simply smiled at his outburst. For a moment he felt unaccountably happy – if she wasn't standing up for that twerp any more, perhaps she'd gone off him at last. Then he saw

107

something else in her eyes and his face fell again. 'You didn't take Simon, did you?' he asked, steadily.

'No,' Caroline said, and for a second he saw that gooey look she'd had on her face in the coffee bar again. 'I didn't go with Simon – I went with Melvin.'

Jeremy nearly exploded. Melvin? Creepo of the year? Zits the size of walnuts? Breath that could drop a rhino at sixty paces? Surely not? 'Er – which Melvin was that, Caroline?' he asked, choking on his coffee.

'Melvin, you know, *the* Melvin, *our* Melvin, the one that works here!' Caroline told him impatiently.

Jeremy gawped at her. 'You mean you . . . and he . . . went out . . . together?'

'What's the matter with you today, Jeremy?' Caroline asked tetchily. 'You're being even slower than usual! Yes – Melvin and I – him and me – himself and myself – went to the ball together, side by side, in tandem, as a pair, whatever you like – *compris*? Am I talking slowly enough for you? Would you like me to write it down or has it sunk into that thick skull of yours at last?'

Jeremy felt sick – he was having enough trouble controlling the odd pang of jealousy he felt when Simon's name kept coming up, but a strict diet of chatting up birds down the pub every night and a constant reminder of how Caroline would look in hockey gear had kept him more or less on the straight and narrow. But this! Fancying Caroline was enough of a cross to bear, but actually feeling jealous of Melvin at the same time was more than either flesh or blood could stand!

With a deep sigh, Jeremy stood up and walked across the office. As if on cue, the door opened and Dottie's secretary appeared, framed in the doorway

108

like a messenger from hell. 'Jeremy,' she announced, 'Dottie wants to have a word with you – in her office – NOW!'

Jeremy paused. He'd been waiting for this summons since arriving back from Scotland, and it couldn't've come at a more appropriate time. With a wry smile and a little wave to an open-mouthed Caroline, he set off to meet his doom, trotting happily after the secretary like a lamb to the slaughter.

Terence eyed Seraphina over his pint of Special Brew. She had to be feeling guilty about something or she'd've dragged him off to the health food bar for a pint of carrot juice instead of quietly agreeing to have lunch in the pub. Testing the water, he bit a large chunk out of the veal and ham pie he'd ordered, but to his alarm she just sighed and took another sip of her Perrier. Worried at last, he tried to chew the food in his mouth, but it tasted of cardboard and he swallowed it whole instead.

'I didn't mean to laugh at you,' he told Seraphina, watching her jingle the ice around in her glass. 'It's just that the whole thing was so ridiculous! I don't know who told you that version of what went on up in Scotland, but it was so far from the truth that it made me roll up, that's all! Honestly, Seraphina, if you could've seen me up there, shivering in some old horse-blanket with only Jerry and about a hundred spiders for company, you'd know how stupid the whole story was! Who told you we'd been chasing three half-naked models about the moors?'

Seraphina looked at him with her ice-blue eyes. 'My mother,' she said, simply. 'And who was it spoke to you on the phone from Italy and gave you the impression

I was out whooping it up every night?' she asked Terence.

'Your mother,' he said, staring back.

'Shake?' Seraphina asked, smiling.

'Shake,' Terence said, taking her hand and holding on to it long after the handshake was over.

'I missed you,' Seraphina told him, beaming as he kissed each of her fingers in turn.

'Not half as much as I missed you!' Terence said huskily, his eyes closing with relief. 'Old Jeremy comes a very poor second on an icy-cold night in the middle of the moors! I'd even've given up my horse-blanket to've had you up there to keep me company and share my porridge! Let's stick together next time, eh? We don't get on very well when we're split up, do we?'

Seraphina nodded in agreement. 'Even Italy seemed boring while I was by myself,' she told him. 'I couldn't wait to get back to grimy, rainy old London to be with you again.'

Suddenly Terence stared hard at his pint. 'Look, Seraphina,' he said, 'I know this is going to sound corny, and I know old Geraldine'll probably have a fit if she finds out, but if it puts a stop to all her interfering it won't be a bad thing.'

'What won't?' Seraphina asked, wondering what he could be talking about.

'Well,' Terence said, taking a deep breath and clutching his glass for support, 'I wondered whether we could . . . sort of . . . get engaged . . . sort of thing, something like that.'

'Get engaged?' Seraphina asked. 'To be married?'

Terence looked worried. 'Yeah, well, that's usually the idea,' he said. 'A bit old-fashioned, I know, but I

110

don't see why we shouldn't start a new trend – after all Geldof did it twice so it can't be that bad!'

For a moment there was total silence in the pub and Terence wondered just how many people were listening. *About the same number who'll hear her turn me down in a minute, I suppose,* he thought gloomily, hoping Seraphina wouldn't laugh out loud as she did it.

'Once would be enough for me,' she said suddenly.

'Once what?' Terence asked, confused.

'Getting married – once should do!' she repeated.

'To me?' Terence asked, grabbing her hand again.

'Well, I can't think of anyone else who's asked me in the last few minutes!' Seraphina said, smiling gently.

Terence grinned. 'You understand this arrangement must not interfere with my career prospects, Miss Foster-Brown?' he asked. 'I must be allowed to continue with my job and use the skills and talents it has taken me so long to learn!'

'Absolutely!' Seraphina agreed, laughing. 'We'll need the pin-money to supplement my own income for the time being, but as soon as I get my break I shall expect to keep you in the manner to which you are accustomed, Terry!'

Laughing, Terence kissed her and stood up from the table. 'This needs champagne!' he announced, moving towards the bar, but Seraphina pulled him back quickly. 'Not for me, Terry,' she said, anxiously. 'I'll stick to mineral water – I don't think champagne agrees with me, somehow!'

'I've got the sack!' Jeremy announced, walking into the office with his hands pushed into his pockets. 'Dottie's just read me the riot act for causing that

111

fiasco in Scotland, and at the end of it all she told me she was giving me the push. Can't say I blame her, really – those models did manage to run up quite a bill at that hotel they booked into, and the whole thing's got to be shot again in a few days' time.'

Caroline watched him sadly. 'But you're such a good writer,' she said, 'it doesn't seem fair! Surely the magazine can afford to run up the odd hotel bill here and there – look at the sort of money they spend when they go off shooting abroad for a few weeks! They normally pay out hundreds of pounds and no one so much as queries the expenses!'

'The accountants have started telling every department to cut right down,' Geraldine Foster-Brown said, butting in. She'd heard Jeremy announcing his dismissal from across the office and she was so delighted she had to rush over straight away. That left only one fly in the ointment when it came to her daughter's chances of getting the permanent job at *Visage*, and now she'd got Terence out of her hair she would have more time to deal with Caroline.

'You really were stupid though, Jeremy,' she added. 'But if you've got the sack, why are you smiling? You did say you'd been given your marching orders, didn't you?' she asked, worriedly.

'Oh yes, Geraldine, I'm off,' Jeremy told her, 'but I won't exactly be shedding any tears.'

'Well, I'm sorry we're such an awful bunch to work with that you can't wait to leave!' Geraldine said, indignant. 'You won't find it very easy to get another job out there, Jeremy!' she added, waggling her finger like a school marm. 'You won't just be able to waltz out of a job like this and into something just as good, you know.'

'Yes I will!' Jeremy told her, beaming.

'What d'you mean?' Caroline asked. 'You know how many interviews you'd been on when I first met you – where are you going to go now?'

'It was just one of those many thousands and millions of interviews that has finally come up trumps!' Jeremy said, pulling a piece of paper out of his pocket. 'With impeccable timing, I hasten to add, or I might just've been flinging my bod out of that window behind you, to join the prostrate corpses of all the other young men Dottie has fired over the years on the tarmac below!'

Geraldine snorted. 'What sort of a job have you landed, Jeremy?' she asked. 'Tea-boy on *The Times*, or something? Nothing that includes organizing fashion shoots in Scotland, I should hope, or I'll be sending the poor unsuspecting cretins a reference off in the next post! You should have a government health warning stamped across you, you know!'

Caroline snatched the letter out of Jeremy's hand. 'Here – I recognize that logo!' she said, brushing away the biscuit crumbs that fell out as she unfolded the notepaper.

'*Dear Baz,*' it read, '*Have finally got the bread together to accomplish a 100% increase in staffing-levels. Would therefore be obliged if you could turn up for some hard graft as soon as convenient to yourself. See you – Rocky.*'

'Rocky!' Caroline yelled. 'That ape-man? Surely you're not going to work for him?'

'This letter is addressed to someone called "Baz",' Geraldine said. 'The job hasn't been offered to you at all!'

113

Caroline sniggered. 'I think you'd better explain,' she told Jeremy.

Caroline had first met Jeremy at an interview for Rocky's pop magazine, and he'd turned up calling himself Baz and doing what he called 'dressing to impress'. Kitted out like a punk, complete with multi-coloured spiked hair, she'd hardly recognized him when he'd walked into *Visage* on the same day wearing a smart suit and a college-boy haircut. Now it seemed Rocky wanted him after all.

'I'm dead chuffed,' Jeremy said. 'This job'll be right up my street!'

'And then there were two . . .' Geraldine Foster-Brown muttered under her breath, thinking about her daughter's job and spotting Seraphina as she rushed into the office behind Jeremy.

'Guess what?' Seraphina yelled, flushed with excitement and happiness, and unfortunately not noticing Geraldine who was lurking behind her. Suspecting that her wildest dreams had all come true on the same wonderful day, Geraldine leapt out to grab her daughter by the arm.

'You got the job?' she screamed. 'Dottie told you at last? Oh, darling, I'm so proud of you! Just think how that awful man would've held you back – I'm so glad you ditched him at last! Now you know I've been right all along!'

Seraphina's smile froze and she looked at her mother with a puzzled expression. 'Job? What job?' she asked. 'Who's got the job?'

Geraldine recoiled in horror.

'Jeremy?' Seraphina asked, seeing his beaming smile. 'Did Dottie give you the job after all?'

'No,' Jeremy announced proudly, 'she gave me the

114

sack! But look at this!' and he threw an arm around Seraphina's shoulders and held the letter up under her nose.

'Jeremy! That's fantastic!' she yelled. 'A rock magazine, eh? Be off interviewing all those famous pop stars, then? I'm so pleased for you!' and she planted a big smacking kiss on his cheek. Jeremy blushed and looked down at his feet.

'So what's your good news, Seraphina?' Caroline asked. 'If it's not about the job or anything.'

Seraphina looked across at her mother and paused, knowing how she'd take the news, but realizing she'd gone too far now to back down. Everyone was looking at her expectantly. 'It's Terry and I,' she said, glowing with happiness, 'we're . . .' but the telephone cut her off in mid-sentence.

'It's for you,' Jeremy announced after listening to a voice on the other end. 'I think it's Terry!'

'Terry?' Seraphina said, smiling into the mouthpiece. 'I was just about to tell every . . .' but Terence's voice sounded so harsh that it sent an icy shudder down the length of her spine.

'I'm in the studio,' he said. 'There's somebody here who's waiting to see you. I think you'd better get down here, Seraphina, and I think you'd better get down here FAST!'

11

Now Now, Not Ever – Never!

Seraphina muttered to herself impatiently as she waited for the lift to arrive. As soon as the doors slid silently open she shot inside, punching the button to the basement and hopping from one foot to the other as it made its seemingly-slow descent. Terence must've had some awful accident – she could tell something was dreadfully wrong by the tone of his voice. She'd never heard him sound like that before. She pictured him lying electrocuted on the studio floor, then remembered that he had made the phone call, so that cut that idea out!

Perhaps he crawled to the phone before he passed out, she thought, chewing her knuckles as she watched the dial at the top of the lift. But why did he waste his last few breaths on her? He hadn't phoned to declare undying love – in fact he'd sounded quite cold and remote – so why hadn't he done the practical thing and phoned for an ambulance instead?

The thought of him slumped over his tripod with the dead phone dangling helplessly from one hand brought a loud sob from the back of her throat and she flew down the corridor so quickly that she had trouble braking on the bends, piling into the tea trolley on the first corner and mowing Melvin down on the second.

'Melvin!' she shouted once she'd recognized the writhing form at her feet. 'Where's Terry? Is he OK? What's happened – TELL ME!'

Melvin blinked. If anyone around there was not OK

it was him, not Terence! He felt his nose to see if it had been broken – in a way he hoped it had, it might make him look even more like Marlon Brando! Disappointed to find it mainly intact – apart from one small spot that appeared to have burst in the struggle – Melvin shrugged miserably. 'Dunno!' he said. 'He was in the studio last time I saw him, which must've been about four and a half minutes ago – maybe five. He looked alright then, but who knows – "in the midst of life", and all that!'

Melvin watched Seraphina closely, impressed by the fear and concern he saw etched across her beautiful face. If this was Terry's new technique for pulling the birds it seemed to be working a treat! Making a mental note to try putting a panicky phone call through to Caroline and wait until she came flying down to see if he was intact, he picked up his camera and shuffled off, rattling it near his ear to check it was OK for the next job.

Seraphina ran into the studio to find it strangely quiet and deserted. Pacing about anxiously, she finally caught sight of Stuart Crystal, the make-up artist, unpacking his brushes in one corner, and she rushed over to find out what was going on.

'Terence?' Stuart asked, puzzled. 'He's OK – I think! We're doing a fashion shoot today and he was just pottering around as usual, getting all the lights sorted out and everything.'

'You didn't see a bright flash or hear a loud bang that might've been him electrocuting himself, did you?' Seraphina asked, relaxing a bit now there was no obvious sign of a bloodbath.

Stuart laughed. 'Well, he always was a bit flash, dear!' he said, digging Seraphina in the ribs. 'But I don't think he's gone up in smoke yet! Look – the model only arrived a little while ago, maybe Terry's in there. I thought I could hear them chatting.'

Seraphina walked across to the changing room and pulled the door open. The sight that greeted her made her reel back in horror. Dolf stood in front of the make-up mirror, stripped to the waist and looking twice as bronzed and handsome as ever. As Seraphina stared in shocked surprise, he crossed the room in two strides and enveloped her in his strong brown arms, covering her mouth with his own and kissing her until she thought she might die of suffocation.

'Zere you are!' he said finally. 'More beautiful even zan ven ve last said goodbye! I haff been vaiting down here for vat seems like a livetime! I zought you ver neffer going to arrive! You are surprised to see me – no?'

Seraphina tried to push him away, looking around in alarm. 'Dolf!' she shouted once she'd found her voice again. 'What on earth are you doing in England? What are you doing here, come to that?'

'I am ze model – no? So I come here to model. *Visage* iz ze most famous magazine – I haff been booked to do ze fashion spread. Ven I vas realizing I vould see you again I vas even more offer ze moon! Now ve can – how you say it? – take up vere ve lefft off – no?'

'No!' Seraphina shouted quickly. 'Look, Dolf, you must understand. I can't see you over here. I already have a boyfriend – we have just become engaged to be married. His name is Terry and he works here too. You mustn't let him think we were serious about one another in Italy. You know we only went out a couple of times!'

Dolf seemed to be wracking his brains. Words like 'engaged' and 'serious' were way above his head when it came to translations because he was still trying to smother her in kisses. One word, however, seemed to have rung a bell. 'Terry?' he asked, thinking for a moment. 'Ah – Terence! Ze photograffer viz whom I vork! Ya – nice man, ve haff talked for a long time!'

'Talked?' Seraphina asked suspiciously. 'What about?'

'You, my darling,' Dolf said happily. 'Vat else? I tell him how besotted ve are viff one anozzer and how many hours off ecstacy ve share in Italy. He vas so happy for us und zat ve find one anozzer again zat he insist on calling you down from ze office in which you vork!'

'Where did he go then?' Seraphina asked desperately. 'Where is he?'

Dolf shrugged. 'I don't know,' he told her. 'I expect he vas realizing ve vould be vanting to be alone – no?' and he lunged at her again.

Dodging out of the way, Seraphina tore out of the studio and set off to find Terence. Once outside she tried all the pubs within staggering distance, drawing a blank at each one until she stumbled inside 'The Squinting Pig'. For a moment she thought the place was deserted after the lunch-time rush, but then she saw the tall, dark-haired figure crouched low in one corner of the bar. 'Terry?' she said quietly, and he spun round to look at her, eyes blazing.

'Terry – let me explain!' she said, her eyes filling with tears at the cold expression on his face.

'Explain?' he said in a deep voice that cracked with emotion. 'Explain what? I think I've just been told the entire story. Or was there something that Dolf the

Dreamboat might've missed out? Some little detail of your love life in Italy that he didn't paint in quite graphic enough detail? Spare me the really intimate bits, Seraphina – I think I've got the gist!' and he turned back to his drink, leaving Seraphina shivering on the spot.

'Love life? Details?' she said. 'What on earth has he been telling you?'

'More than I wanted to hear, that's for sure!' Terence said, rubbing his hand over his face. 'Stuart Crystal seemed to find the whole conversation quite fascinating, though – I suppose he's spreading it half-way round the building by now!'

'He was unpacking his kit in the studio when I last saw him, Terry,' Seraphina said. 'What Dolf told you sounds like a load of lies – we had dinner a couple of times, that's all! There was nothing serious between the two of us!'

'Look at the bloke, Seraphina,' Terence said. 'He's like a walking Adonis – perfection on two legs! Why would that Hunk from Hamburg have to go around making up girlfriends he doesn't have? Why would he feel he had to come jetting across Europe just to make *me* feel jealous? We'd never even met before today! I suppose you're going to tell me this is all still part of some dastardly plot your mother's been hatching again! Well, if that's what it is, I take my hat off to her this time – she's excelled herself, she really has!'

At the mention of her mother, Seraphina suddenly snapped back to life. Certain things started to slot into certain holes and a couple of loose ends started to tie themselves up. She suddenly remembered the smell of Geraldine's perfume on the opera tickets, and thought of all the strange coincidences that had happened, from Dolf making a bee-line towards her at the fashion show to the way he just happened to have a booking with the magazine for a fashion spread. She remembered how they seemed to have had just about everything in common – tastes in food, tastes in music, views on everything from politics to pig-farming – and suddenly it all seemed just a bit too snug for comfort. Warning lights started to flash in front of her eyes, and she hardly heard Terence's next words.

'I want the ring back,' he said.

'The ring?' Seraphina asked him. 'You didn't buy me an engagement ring!'

Terence fished in his coat pocket and pulled out a small box. 'Yes I did,' he said sadly. 'I just didn't have a chance to give it to you, that's all.'

Seraphina opened the box and looked at the ring. It was perfect – a small white-gold band with one single diamond embedded in the gold. 'Thanks,' she said. 'It's lovely,' and she handed it back to Terence again.

'Good,' he said, taking it. 'I knew you'd like it. Shame.'

'Yes,' Seraphina said, 'shame,' and she walked out of the wine bar before she broke down altogether.

12
Hanging On

'I'm sorry you're leaving,' Caroline told Jeremy as they sorted through the clothes from the last fashion shoot, bagging them up for the motorcycle messenger to take back to the appropriate fashion houses.

'Whose is this?' she asked, holding up a particularly ugly-looking peaked hat.

'Head Start,' Jeremy told her, 'Great Portland Street – put it in with those orange gloves over there. I think they're from the same place.

'No you're not!' he added, suddenly.

'Why not?' Caroline asked, surprised. 'I like working with you – it's fun!'

Fun! Jeremy thought. Only Caroline would use a word like that about him – it made it sound as though they'd just played a game of hockey together! None of his other girlfriends ever described him as 'fun'. Stunningly exciting – yes! Sexy, even, but 'fun' – never!

'You can't be sorry to see the back of me, though,' he went on. 'It means you're only up against Seraphina for the job now. Surely that's good news?'

'It's not just the job though, Jeremy,' Caroline said, and he looked up quickly in alarm. Her eyes had gone all gooey again. Jeremy looked round quickly for the emergency exit.

'I mean,' she added, 'we can still see one another, can't we? In a professional capacity, of course?'

Jeremy looked at her again. Somehow, in the right light, with the wind in an easterly direction and if he half-closed one eye, she wasn't bad-looking – beautiful, in fact. 'Yes, of course we can see one another – in a professional capacity – sometimes,' he said. There was silence as they rooted through the clothes again.

'When . . . er . . . when do you think this first professional capacity might be?' Jeremy asked nervously.

'Oooh . . . er . . . let's see,' Caroline said, scratching her head. 'I should imagine Wednesday night, or thereabouts!'

'Fine, fine,' Jeremy agreed soberly. 'And . . . er . . . whereabouts do you think we ought to be having this business discussion, then?'

Caroline looked thoughtful again. 'Screen On The Green?' she said eventually. 'I hear they've got a very good season of late-night horror films on there this month!'

'Perfect!' Jeremy said, and they both dissolved into laughter. Caroline stuck the horrible hat on top of Jeremy's head and he retaliated by wrapping an enormous studded bra around her head and over her eyes, like a blindfold. When the phone rang it made them both jump and Jeremy hooted with laughter as he watched Caroline play 'Blind-man's-bluff' looking for it. When she finally found it Dottie's voice from the other end had her jumping to her feet with fright.

'It was Dottie,' she told Jeremy, looking pale. 'She wants me in the office in two minutes – says she's finally made her decision about the job.'

Jeremy unwound the bra and kissed her on the cheek. 'Off you go, kiddo,' he said. 'It's make or break time. Good luck!' and he propelled the rather worried-looking Caroline out of the door and down the corridor to Dottie's office.

123

Once inside, Caroline was rather surprised to see Seraphina already sitting there. Her eyes looked red-rimmed as though she'd just been crying, and for one moment Caroline thought she must've already been told she hadn't got the job. Then Dottie beamed at both of them and she realized Seraphina knew as little as she did.

'I won't beat around the bush,' Dottie began. 'I know you both want to know what's going to happen and I don't want to prolong the agony any longer than I have to. You've both worked hard, and the only reason I didn't make a decision earlier was because it was too difficult to choose between you. Now Jeremy will be leaving us and my problem has been made a little easier. Caroline,' she said, turning to face her, 'you're my choice for the permanent job – you work hard and the other staff say you're easy to get on with. The scoop with the princess helped sway the balance, of course, but that was a one-off, and the important part of your job here will be that you can assist the other writers, rather than be too much of a star turn in your own right. You do understand that, don't you? You've got a long way to go before you start getting ambitious, and until then your job is just to keep your head down and be as helpful as possible – OK?'

Caroline nodded – she could hardly believe what she was hearing. In between the lectures and warnings, Dottie was offering her the permanent job! Ripples of excitement started to work their way up her body, but then she remembered Seraphina and her smile froze. Geraldine would never forgive her for not getting the job. Caroline looked at her friend with sympathy, but Dottie interrupted her before she could speak.

'Seraphina,' Dottie said, 'you're a good writer, but

as I've just explained to Caroline, that wasn't all I was looking for. I liked that article you did on animal liberation and I liked the way you worked on your own initiative. The magazine needs young writers like you, but it can't afford to carry you along while you're training, despite rumours of the enormous budgets we work on. I can't go into details, but you'll have to take my word for it when I tell you if I could afford to keep you on I would. Unfortunately we're cutting down and my hands have been tied. What really annoys me is the fact that you'll go and get a job on some other magazine and they'll reap the benefits of your talent while we couldn't afford to keep you. However,' she went on, leaning back in her chair and peering hard at Seraphina, 'I think things may be changing around here very shortly, and I want to give you the option of still being around to see if there are any openings then. Half my staff are taking their holidays over the next couple of months and I can use that as an excuse to keep you on a bit longer. If you'd rather leave and start looking around for another job I'll quite under-stand, but if you want to stay on I'll be delighted. What d'ya say?'

Seraphina looked at Caroline and she looked over at Dottie. Stay? Of course she'd stay – and she'd hang on tooth and nail and fight her way back with every ounce of energy she had. Nodding at Dottie she leapt up from her chair and hugged Caroline, smiling happily. First she'd sort out things with her mother, then she'd work her way to the best job on the magazine. Somehow on the way she'd get Terry back again, too – she didn't care how hard she'd have to fight to win him round! Smiling to herself, she looked down at her left hand and admired the white-gold engagement ring for the umpteenth time. Terry had been too miserable to notice she'd given him back an empty box, and when he finally found out and came to get the ring back she'd start working things out between them. Chattering happily, the two girls set off down the corridor to find Jeremy and break the good news to him first – at last they were all going to be writers!

Colour illustrated storybooks for the young reader

Help Your Child to Read
Allan Ahlberg and Eric Hill

Fast Frog	85p	☐
Bad Bear	85p	☐
Double Ducks	85p	☐
Poorly Pig	85p	☐
Rubber Rabbit	85p	☐
Silly Sheep	85p	☐

Allan Ahlberg and André Amstutz

Mister Wolf	85p	☐
Travelling Moose	85p	☐
Hip-Hippo Ray	85p	☐
King Kangaroo	85p	☐
Tell-Tale Tiger	85p	☐
Spider Spy	85p	☐

Help Your Child to Count
Richard & Nicky Hales and André Amstutz

Slimy Slugs	95p	☐
Captain Caterpillar	95p	☐
Furry Foxes	95p	☐
Boris Bat	95p	☐
Panda Picnic	95p	☐
Froggy Football	95p	☐

Rub A Dub Dub
Alan Rogers

Yankee Doodle	95p	☐
Three Men in a Tub	95p	☐
One for the Money	95p	☐
Tom, Tom the Piper's Son	95p	☐
Hey Diddle Diddle	95p	☐
Poor Old Robinson Crusoe	95p	☐

To order direct from the publisher just tick the titles you want and fill in the order form.